The Coldest
Winter

The Coldest Winter

ELIZABETH LUTZEIER

Holiday House / New York

First published in Great Britain by Oxford University Press
First published in the United States of America by Holiday House, Inc., 1991

Library of Congress Cataloging-in-Publication Data
Lutzeier, Elizabeth.
The coldest winter / by Elizabeth Lutzeier.
p.   cm.
Summary: When the potato blight ruins the food crop in 1846
and English soldiers start turning people out of their homes,
Eamonn and his family struggle to survive through the
coldest winter Ireland has ever known.
ISBN 0-8234-0899-X
[1. Victims of famine—Fiction.   2. Ireland—Fiction.]   I. Title.
PZ7.L979554Co   1991   91-7159   CIP   AC
[Fic]—dc20

For
Jenny and Denis Byrne,
who never deserted me

1

The Eviction

The soldier shrugged his shoulders and smiled. He didn't understand. Eamonn's mother was shouting and crying loud enough for people in the next village to hear her, but from where he was standing, on the far side of the road, Eamonn could see that the soldier didn't understand a single word of what she was trying to tell him. None of the English soldiers could speak Irish.

Eamonn's father couldn't help. He was right over at the opposite end of the square near O'Malley's house. The big hefty brutes with crowbars who always came to an eviction with the soldiers were smashing away at the O'Malleys' walls with their sledge hammers and hacking at the thatched roof with pickaxes. They wouldn't have needed to use such force. The house collapsed like a pile of soft sand.

When he stood on tiptoe, Eamonn could just make out the figure of Mrs O'Malley, crying and still lying on the ground where the soldiers had left her when they flung her out of their way. Eamonn's mother had given him the job of watching over the little ones, though he was the only boy left with the group of women and children. From where he was standing it looked as if all the men and boys of Ballinglas were crowded round the soldiers, shouting and kicking, pulling at their sleeves and trying to get them to leave the roof alone.

'Don't tumble the roof!' Eamonn recognized his father's voice in among all the shouting. 'For pity's sake! The man's got five children. Leave him a roof over his head.'

Either the men with the crowbars weren't able to speak Irish, or else someone had put a spell on them, freezing their hearts so that they couldn't feel any pity for the children who were going to have to sleep out in the cold fields. None of them paid any attention to the shouting, hacking away at the roof of the house as if it were some fierce animal they had to kill. They were big men, bigger than the soldiers some of them, with red faces, bruised and brutal.

Eamonn wondered at the size of them. What was it that made them so big and brawny when no one around Galway had had anything to eat but a handful of turnips for months? Did the British army keep a special food supply for their labourers, just so they'd be strong enough to go round tumbling the houses when there was an eviction?

There was so much happening all at once. Eamonn glanced over to their house where his mother was standing, still desperately trying to argue with the soldier. Didn't she see how useless it was to argue with someone who didn't speak her language?

He felt stupid, just waiting on the other side of the road looking after his little brothers and baby sister. He thought he ought to be doing something more to help in the fight when those big bullies were getting ready to tear down his house. It wasn't right to stand there and do nothing when he could see the way the soldier kept on pushing his mother away from their door, ignoring her cries. His only consolation was that the soldier wasn't being rough with his mother, not like the big sergeant who had thrown Mrs O'Malley down into the dirt.

The one outside their cabin was a small man with a neat moustache who tried to smile at Eamonn's mother while he kept on shaking his head. He stood rigidly to attention in front of their door, with both arms stretched out, preventing her from going back into the house. Eamonn handed the baby to Dermot and warned him to stay where he was and keep an eye on Shaun.

'She only wants a blanket!' he shouted, racing over to the soldier. 'You can let her go back in to get a blanket for the baby, can't you? We've only got the one. My brother forgot to bring it out with him.'

The soldier grinned. 'I never knew no one round here could speak the Queen's English. Here.' He lifted up his arm. 'You nip in and get it, but don't let no one see you.'

He looked scared and kept glancing over to the other side of the square, where the sergeant in charge was dragging great chunks of thatch from the O'Malleys' roof. 'Tell your mam she'd better carry on screaming, so's they won't know anything about it. I'm not supposed to let anyone back in, you know.'

It was dark in the cabin, even darker than usual because there were no windows and the soldier was standing at the door, blocking out the daylight. But Eamonn could have found everything in the cabin with his eyes closed.

He skirted round the last glowing embers of the turf fire and found the baby's blanket and two of his father's books. It was so warm inside their cabin. Eamonn wished he could curl up by the fire and go to sleep. Not half an hour ago, they had all been sitting there in the warmth, his Grandma, Mammy and Daddy and the three little ones. It would be so nice to go to sleep and pretend that what was happening outside was all a bad dream.

He tried to ignore the women screaming and the frightened neighing of the horses as soldiers rode them into the groups of men who were still protesting about the evictions.

But Eamonn knew it was no good going to sleep; they would tumble the house on top of him and then they wouldn't let him rescue anything. They would make him go out into the cold without even a blanket for the baby.

He wrapped his father's books up in the blanket and

crept out of the cabin from underneath the soldier's arm. No one was looking in his direction. Most of the soldiers and all the big men with their axes and crowbars had moved on to the next cabin, where the Nolans lived.

Mr and Mrs Nolan weren't even bothering to fight with the soldiers. They had rescued a little pile of books and a bundle of clothes and stood watching quietly while the rough men grunted and cursed whenever they reached a bit of wall which didn't obligingly collapse as soon as they hit it. It didn't take them long to destroy a house.

Eamonn was old enough to remember the big party they had had in the village when everyone helped to build Mr Nolan's house. They had all been so pleased to have a schoolteacher at last in Ballinglas that someone had killed a pig and there had been a feast the whole weekend while the men worked on making it the finest house of any schoolmaster in the district. The Nolans' house had had two windows, with painted wooden shutters to keep out the cold. Now the pickaxes ripped through the wood with a sound like scissors cutting through silk.

Eamonn took the blanket back to the others and sat in the ditch again, straining to catch the words his father and the other men aimed at the soldiers.

'We paid our rent on time!' Mr O'Malley picked up a stone to throw at the men who were tearing down the Nolans' house, but the soldiers had guns and no one knew when they might use them. Someone caught hold of his hand just in time. 'She's no right to turn us out when we've paid our rent,' he shouted, flinging the useless stone far away from him out into the empty field.

The angry words the men shouted were like a hail of blunt arrows. The soldiers didn't understand them. And even if they had been able to speak Irish it wasn't their job to pay attention to the Irish tenant farmers. Mrs

Gerrard wanted her land back and the British soldiers were there with their guns and their horses to get it back for her. Her agent had told her she would make more money if she put sheep out to pasture there, where two hundred people lived. She never thought to ask him where the families would go to after they had been turned off her land.

Mr Nolan had thought he could speak to her and tell her what would happen if she went ahead and evicted all the families of Ballinglas from their homes. But she lived in England most of the time. She was only ever at home in the big house during the summer, when she had English visitors who went fishing for salmon.

The villagers had tried talking to her agent, but he didn't listen to them. He just shrugged his shoulders and said the same things over and over again. 'I can see your problem,' he used to say, and they all began to hope that perhaps they might persuade him to let them stay. But then he carefully explained that unless Mrs Gerrard started using the land for something else she would be ruined, and then where would they be? 'You certainly wouldn't be better off than you are now, if Mrs Gerrard went bankrupt. And I'd be out of a job as well.'

Eamonn walked back across the field to their cabin. The soldier guarding their door looked down at the ground as Eamonn approached. He was ashamed of himself and angry with the British Army. Ever since he'd arrived in Ireland with the 49th Infantry he'd done nothing but march round the country evicting people. He still hadn't got used to the idea. He kept wondering what he would feel like if someone threw his mother out of her cottage in England, or his sister, living all alone with her three children. He hated the way some of the soldiers beat the women to make them keep away from their houses when there was an eviction. The sergeant in charge wasn't such a rough man with the soldiers, but it was obvious he couldn't stand the way the women sobbed and pulled at his uniform and begged him to leave their cabins alone. That must be why he hit them and pushed them out of his way. He didn't want to have to listen to their crying. No one liked evictions. It was dirty work, but they had their orders. It had to be done.

The soldier sighed and then grinned at Eamonn. 'You must be a smart lad, if you can speak English. Where d'you pick that up, then?'

'At school.' Eamonn wasn't sure if his parents would think it was right to start chatting to one of the English soldiers who was helping to turn them out of their home.

He looked round. His mother was sitting on the ground on the other side of the road, holding the baby and rocking her backwards and forwards, forwards and backwards, every time she heard the noises of the crowbars biting into the Nolans' house. His father was still protesting, caught up in the crowd of villagers who were all shouting in the language no one wanted to understand.

'I got English at school from Mr Nolan,' Eamonn said, nodding in the direction of the schoolteacher.

Mr Nolan had his arm round his wife and watched quietly as the soldiers stamped on the last traces of his house, as people watch quietly when a coffin is being lowered into the ground at a funeral.

The soldier laughed. 'I never saw no school round here. Where's your school, then?'

Eamonn pointed to the tumbled house, where the men were stamping all over the ruins, making sure that nothing could be salvaged from the wreckage.

'We had school in Mr Nolan's house,' he said. 'And when it was fine we sat outside in the sun and did our learning. I liked that best. They were going to build a proper schoolhouse here next year, with benches for the children to sit on, because Mr Nolan wanted to stay.

But now you've taken away his house and he's going to live with his brother in America.'

The soldier whistled and frowned. They were pushing women down with their rifles again. It was a bad job. If he told people back in England what they had to do when they were on duty in Ireland no one would believe him. He didn't want to think of what was going to happen to all the people. He'd seen enough poor beggars out on the roads already, and now there were going to be two hundred more people with nowhere to go.

'You wouldn't have kept me in a little mud cabin like that,' he joked. 'They needed a proper schoolhouse to keep me in. Dirty great big walls it had and even then I escaped whenever I could. I was glad when me Dad said he wanted me out at work, so I didn't have to go to school no more. I used to hide every morning so they wouldn't make me go.'

Eamonn had never met anyone who didn't want to go to school. 'My Dad didn't have any kind of schoolhouse,' he said. 'When he went to school they all hid behind a hedge, so's the English wouldn't see them. They didn't want Irish boys to have any schooling then. So the priest taught them behind the hedge.'

'Ah, well, that's why he can't speak English,' the soldier said. 'Them priests can't speak no English. I've never met anyone who can speak English round here, not till you came along. Now over in Dublin it's different. You ought to go to Dublin one day. It's a nice place. Posh shops and that.'

The soldier put his arms down. They were beginning to ache from standing all that time trying to guard the door.

'The priest didn't speak English,' Eamonn said, 'but he taught our Daddy to speak Latin.'

The soldier laughed, 'Latin, eh?' That was a joke he'd have to tell them back home. An Irish peasant in a miserable, run-down cabin miles from anywhere says he can speak Latin, just like a scholar. That'd give them a laugh.

Suddenly everything became much quieter. Ten houses were already gone and the people had realized that there was nothing they could do. They were poor and hungry, with no weapons, while the soldiers had rifles with bayonets and the big strong men had their crowbars and pickaxes. All of them were well-fed too.

The women and children were sitting together on the far side of the road, away from the village. The men round Eamonn's father drew slowly back from the next house that the vandals had started to tear down. Some of the tiny children were crying, but everyone else was silent. Nobody knew what to do with their anger. It wasn't right what Mrs Gerrard was doing, but there was nothing they could do to stop her when she had the English soldiers on her side.

'You'd better move out of the way, son, so you don't get hurt.' The soldier caught hold of Eamonn's shoulder as the wrecking gang moved closer to his house. 'There's nothing you can do now.'

Eamonn turned on him, 'Why are you doing this?' He punched the man with his fists. 'Stop them! Why don't you stop them? We don't want to sleep out in the cold. The baby might die. Why don't you stop them?'

The soldier shook his head. He didn't try to stop Eamonn hitting him. The boy had scarcely any strength. 'If we don't do what they say, they put us in jail. And if they put me in jail, there's no money gets sent to my wife. Do you want her to get turned out too?'

The soldier held on to Eamonn's wrists. It came as a shock to feel how thin they were. 'What would you do, if you was me?' he shouted.

Eamonn walked slowly over to the ditch where the women were sitting. His head was battered by his own angry words, trapped inside him because no one would listen to them. It was a cold March day and he had only his shirt and trousers on, but he felt hot. There was a blacksmith's hammer banging at the hot anvil inside his head.

Everything was blurred but he noticed his mother, with her head between her knees, crying quietly, not wanting to look at their house while the soldiers razed it to the ground. Dermot was hopping his knees up and down, bouncing the baby. Eamonn's little brother Shaun was quiet, huddled up to Grandma, who stroked his hair, looking intently at the soldiers near their cabin as if she could stop the men from tearing it down by glaring at them. Eamonn heard some of the women wailing, but their cries seemed to come from a long way off, like the cries he heard when a funeral procession was going through the gap to the graveyard in the mountains.

He was looking towards the hills and had his back to the village, but he knew when the wreckers started on their cabin. Grandma stopped stroking Shaun's hair and made a cross on her forehead. Eamonn noticed how white her hands were, with blue and purple veins, like the finest marble. Shaun buried his head in Grandma's shawl and kept his eyes shut tightly, not making any sound.

Suddenly before anyone could stop her, Eamonn's mother was at their cabin, trying to pull the red-faced sergeant away from the wall that the men were about to demolish. 'The children, sir! My children have nowhere to sleep tonight! Have pity on us, sir!'

The sergeant towered above her. He was big, even for an Englishman, but Eamonn's mother was strong. She managed to hold fast to his arm and stop him wielding the great iron bar that would have smashed the wall down as easily as you smash the top off an egg.

'Don't be stupid, woman!' The sergeant struggled with her, trying to pull his arm free, but she was so desperate that for a few minutes she was stronger than he was.

'Where can I put my children to sleep tonight, sir, if

15

you take away our house? Have pity on us, sir. Don't do this to us.'

The English soldiers knew what she was pleading for, even if none of them could speak Irish. But the sergeant pretended that he couldn't understand her. He had to obey his orders. The village was to be cleared by nightfall.

He let the crowbar fall to the ground and heaved his right arm out of her grip with renewed strength. With the other arm he flung her as far away from himself as he could, making her fall back against the sharp rocks of the wall behind their house and cut her head. Then he turned his attention to the house, picked up the crowbar and made the low roof crash inwards with one mighty blow. Mammy was lying stunned on the ground, but the sergeant never looked at her again.

Eamonn was shaking with anger as he went to help his mother. If someone had given him a gun he would have killed that man.

2

Shelter

As soon as the soldiers had tumbled all the houses they started to move the people away from their village.

Some official back in Cork had given the order that the whole area had to be cleared. It didn't matter that it was March 13th and icy winds became whips lashing at the childrens' bare legs so that they screamed in pain. The soldiers felt the cold even through their thick woollen coats, but to do their job properly they had to forget that poor people could feel the cold as well. They had to pretend they didn't care what the old people would do for a bed that night.

'They're not used to beds, anyway,' the grey-haired sergeant sneered. His red face had turned purple with the cold and he wanted to get the job over with as quickly as he could.

It was true what he said. The Nolans were the only family in the whole village who had ever had enough money to buy a bed; the others had slept huddled together on the floor of their cabins. But they'd at least had a roof over their heads, and most of all, they had been warm.

Eamonn couldn't remember that he had ever been so cold in all his life. He longed for the warm fire in their cabin. He even longed for the smell of the turf smoke that used to sting his eyes when the cabin door was closed against the winter winds. He was used to being hungry, much more hungry than he was now, but at least they had never been cold. At nights, they had cuddled up close together, warmed by the turf fire and his grandmother's stories. In winter they never needed to go out for more than the few minutes it took to dash across to Mr Nolan's, or to fetch turf and collect water from the river. Nobody in the village had the clothes they would have needed to be outdoors in that kind of weather.

The cruel cold beat them until they were purple and blue. People sat by the roadside, shrinking down and sinking their heads into their shoulders, as if that would deceive the wind and make it pass them by. Mr and Mrs Nolan, whose brother had sent them the money to sail to America, had already set off on the long walk to Dublin, but no one else thought of moving on. There was nowhere to go to.

The soldiers grew impatient when the people didn't move. The village had to be cleared by the time the sun went down and it was already four o'clock. Way down the road, they had already started threatening the crowd with their bayonets and some were riding their horses right up to the families sitting on the ground to frighten them.

'Come on, you rabble!' the sergeant was shouting. 'I'm not going to ask no questions. I don't care where you go, just so long as you're off Mrs Gerrard's land tonight. That's our orders. I'm a reasonable man. That's all I'm asking you to do. Get a move on there.'

As the soldiers moved closer with their bayonets, some of the men started to shout again, pushing right up against the sides of the horses. Then the soldiers began to kick out at them with the spurs on their boots and Eamonn saw old Mr Galvin fall back onto the road, pressing his hands against a great gash in his forehead. A frightened horse had reared up and kicked him before anyone knew what was happening. Two soldiers got off their horses and helped him to stand up.

'Come along, sir.' It was the soldier who had been stationed outside Eamonn's cabin before they tore it down. 'You've got to move along now, sir.'

The soldier was as gentle as a nurse with a sick child. He saw Eamonn looking at him. 'This old man is half-starved,' he said. Mr Galvin was white and shaking. He could only stand up as long as the two soldiers were holding both his arms.

'Here.' The soldier held out a coin to Eamonn. 'Buy yourselves something to eat, will you, lad?'

Eamonn took the large, gold coin and examined it. He had no idea how much it was worth because he'd only ever seen money once before, when Mr Nolan showed them some American coins in school. The only money Mr Nolan possessed came from his brother in America, because where Eamonn lived the school-master got paid in kind, not in money. The children used to take him some eggs or a couple of sods of turf to keep his fire burning, in return for their lessons.

'Where shall I buy something?' Eamonn looked back at the devastated village. 'There never were any shops in Ballinglas. There is no food to buy.'

He held out the money, to give it back to the soldier, but the soldier shook his head.

'You'll find somewhere to spend it,' he said. Then, still holding on to Mr Galvin with one hand to stop him falling down, he patted Eamonn's baby sister on the cheek with the other. 'There should be enough to buy something for the little one and the old man as well,' he said.

The sergeant hadn't even noticed what happened when Mr Galvin got kicked by the horse. The soldiers he was with had ridden off down the road just as Mr Galvin fell, chasing another group of people away and leaving the old man alone with Eamonn and the two soldiers who had helped him. Now the main group of soldiers came charging back, their spurs glittering like icicles, their nervous horses snorting and blowing out clouds of mist.

'No loitering,' bellowed the sergeant. 'I have orders to clear this road by tonight. If I let one family stay, they'll all want to stay. So get a move on! Shoo! Be off with you!'

'You'd better get going,' Eamonn's soldier said. 'Good luck. And look after that beautiful baby.'

He mounted his horse and was soon lost in the crowd of soldiers, faces red from the cold, whose only wish was to clear the last few stragglers from Mrs Gerrard's land so they could go back to their barracks and get warm. The horses pawed the ground and stamped nervously while the soldiers waited and kept watch over the boy and the old man, as if the two of them and the baby wrapped in the shawl on Eamonn's chest were about to mount a vicious, armed attack.

They started to walk but their progress was painfully slow. Rosaleen was heavy and Eamonn sometimes had to support the whole weight of the old man when his legs nearly gave way underneath him. Eamonn didn't dare to look back. He felt the eyes of the troop of soldiers like icy water falling, drop by drop, down his back. No one else had dared to look back either. Most of the people walked as quickly as they could, just to keep warm, but Eamonn and old Mr Galvin made very slow progress. When they finally caught up with his family about a mile further down the road his father and mother took hold of the old man's arms and helped him to keep on walking.

'Just a wee bit further now. Then you can rest, old man.' Eamonn's father had a voice that soothed away the old man's pain and made the children forget they were cold. The voice he had used to curse the soldiers when they were trying to drive him out of his home belonged to a different person.

The sun was setting slowly, sinking to rest behind the gap in the hills ahead of them. Every so often, when his father forgot to cheer them up with one of his funny stories, Eamonn noticed the sharp needles of the cold night air pricking into his arms and legs. But at least the wind had died down.

They moved along very slowly, almost in silence, saving their breath to help the old man. In the dusk Eamonn thought he could see a few shadowy figures slipping away over the hills. It was strange, how quickly the other families had disappeared, two hundred people left to find shelter against the bitterly cold March night. Soon Eamonn and his family were the only souls left in the whole of Galway, shuffling along the silent, empty road with old Mr Galvin.

Grandma and his mother walked briskly, taking turns to carry Shaun. Eamonn still had the baby wrapped up in the blanket and tied so tightly around him that he had his hands free to support Mr Galvin.

'We'll be stopping soon, old man.' His father's gentle voice broke the silence like a mountain stream that murmurs every now and then to remind you that the water is still there if you need it. The baby was asleep and Dermot and Shaun were as quiet as they were when a pedlar came to their village, as if they were waiting excitedly to see what the night would pull out of his pack.

Things could have been worse. They had managed to get the blanket, so the baby wouldn't freeze to death. The blanket and little Rosaleen cuddled up against him both helped to keep Eamonn warm. He wondered how Dermot felt. Dermot marched on beside his mother and Grandma, swinging his arms, his thin arms in the thin, cotton shirt.

Dermot didn't look cold and he didn't complain. He kept on walking at a steady pace, staring at the gap in the hills, where the sun was all but gone. Eamonn didn't know how long they were going to keep on walking.

'You might take a turn at carrying Rosaleen, our Dermot.' Eamonn sounded weary, and Dermot stopped without a word to take the baby from him. Then, 'Don't wake her up,' he said. Eamonn wrapped the blanket tightly round his brother so that the baby could curl up, snug and warm, against his chest.

'She's heavy as one of those little pigs Daddy let us raise,' laughed Dermot, and then broke into a run to catch up with his mother.

Fists of cold air suddenly thumped against Eamonn's chest, taking his breath away, and he couldn't fight back. He thought of their cabin and the warm turf fire and the days when they had eaten stirabout every night, porridge so hot that they burned their mouths and Daddy laughed and said it served them right for trying to gulp it down so fast. The cold night was a great cowardly bully who didn't stop hitting you even when you were down. Eamonn wanted to run to Grandma, to cuddle himself warm in her shawl, but she was carrying Shaun. And anyway, she might say he was too big for cuddles, a great big boy of eleven.

The old man started to say something, but at first no one could understand him. He didn't have enough breath in his body to speak out loud. Eamonn and his father stopped walking but still they could scarcely catch what he was whispering.

'What's he saying?' Grandma turned round and hitched Shaun up over her shoulder. She was a tough little woman who would walk all day if you asked her to. She didn't think much of the English, and she certainly didn't intend to let a few English soldiers spoil her peace. But she looked worried. All of them could see that things looked bad with the old man. They stopped and crowded round him.

'I think he means he wants to lie down here,' said Dermot. 'He's too tired to walk any more.'

Mr Galvin nodded. His long thin legs kept buckling underneath him and Eamonn and his father had to struggle to stop him falling. He breathed out more words, which only Dermot could understand.

'He thinks if we just leave him to rest here for the night he'll be able to walk to the poorhouse on his own tomorrow morning. They'll have to take him in,' said Dermot, nodding.

Dermot had big blue eyes and his face had got so thin since the potatoes had all gone rotten that his eyes, as round and solemn as an angel's, were the only thing you noticed about him. 'He doesn't want to hold us up and they can't turn him away at the workhouse if he tells them he has nowhere to go.'

'If we leave him to rest here for the night, there's only one place he'll be going tomorrow and that's up to heaven, God rest his soul.'

Grandma made Shaun stand down on the ground. 'Come on, old man. You lean on me,' she said. 'We'll find a nice warm place for us all to sleep and you'll soon be as right as rain. You're not going to let those Englishes get you down now, are you?'

'There's an old cabin in the Gap,' Eamonn shouted, taking Shaun's hand and running forward a few steps with him. He had just remembered the time he climbed up the hillside and found the cabin while he was out looking for blackberries. 'We won't have far to go, Mr Galvin. It's the old cabin near the graveyard where the priest used to live. They haven't tumbled that, and they won't even think of going up there.'

Eamonn was right. Up on the left side of the hill as you came through the gap was a large cabin. It must have even had windows once, when there was still a priest living near Ballinglas. The people always built a good-sized cabin for the priest, so there were two rooms. Nobody minded that the roof was off on one side of the cabin. They all crowded into the one room that still had most of its roof on, thrilled at their good fortune. There was even a bundle of hay in one corner where they could put Rosaleen down to sleep.

'Hey!' Eamonn's father whirled Grandma round in a wild dance. 'Now you can get warmed up, Grandma,' he said. 'I'll bet you we can make a fire too, if we find a bit of turf. We'll soon be living like lords.'

He went outside, round the back of the house and very shortly came back in with an armful of neatly cut squares of almost dry turf. 'Look at this!' He tried to juggle with four pieces of the turf and dropped them all in a heap on the floor. 'That priest must have left in a hurry! Eamonn and me don't even have any turf cutting to do before we all settle down for the night.'

Grandma had a surprise for them too. She had dug up ten carrots and hidden them in her shawl while most of the soldiers were busy over at the far side of the village. 'There was only that young one standing at our door,' she said. 'He kept babbling on and on at me. I couldn't understand a word he said, but he was smiling. So I let him keep on chattering as long as he let me keep on getting me carrots. I could have got more, only that big bully sergeant was riding over to our side of the village again and I didn't like the look of him.'

Old Mr Galvin didn't want to eat. He lay on the heap of straw next to Rosaleen, already half asleep, while the others sat round the fire, feeling the life return to their frozen toes, warming their hands and eating the deliciously sweet carrots. It felt so good to be out of the cold, so good that Eamonn almost forgot that he could have eaten three or four carrots instead of one.

The children all lay down next to old Mr Galvin to keep him warm, and Grandma cuddled up with the baby. Shaun wanted Mammy to sing him to sleep with some of her old songs, and while she was still singing the others gradually fell asleep as well. Soon, only Eamonn was awake. He listened to his mother and father talking in low voices.

'It could have been much much worse,' his father was saying. 'How many poor unfortunates are out there having to make themselves a shelter in a ditch this night?'

'The old man would surely have died,' his mother said. 'We couldn't have left him by the roadside.'

'No more we won't.' Eamonn's father yawned. 'He's a charge on us now. We'll find a way of looking after him.'

Mammy's voice was like music even when she talked. Eamonn had always begged her to sing him to sleep when he was a little boy like Shaun. 'We are blessed,' she said. 'They won't come looking for us up here. They'll leave us in peace. Do you remember how they hounded out those poor wretches who had to hide in ditches in Killimor? You'd think they wouldn't want to take anything more off you when they've already taken the roof over your head. But they won't come up here, sure they won't.'

The turf fire glowed in the pitch darkness. It was so warm in the cabin, and the scent of the turf fire burning reminded Eamonn of the potatoes they used to bake in the fire the years before the blight came and killed all the potatoes off. The smell of that fire was almost as good as having something to eat.

Eamonn was awoken by the sounds of harnesses jangling and horses stamping and there was a heavy thumping at the door. He thought he was still dreaming of all the bad things that had happened the day before. The fire was glowing and the cabin was warm and dark, but he could see the cracks of daylight where there were holes in the thatched roof. Grandma sat up and grabbed hold of Eamonn's wrist. 'What's that?'

'We can only give you one more warning. This house is going to be tumbled today. Come out before we start if you want to save your skin.'

It was the voice of the grey-haired sergeant.

3

The Grand Canal

If you went along the Grand Canal as far as you could, all the way through Queen's County and beyond, you would eventually get to Dublin. And in Dublin there was work. At least that was what people said. They said that if you got work in the big city you didn't have to have a piece of land to feed your family any more and you didn't have to worry about crops failing. If you worked for one of the rich families in Dublin you could get enough money to pay for a place to live and still have some left over. You could buy so much food that you'd never go hungry again. People back in Galway used to talk about the shops in Dublin where you could just walk in and buy all the food you wanted.

It was hard to believe that there were places where you didn't have to grow your own potatoes to make sure you had enough to eat, places where it didn't matter if the potatoes weren't any good.

Eamonn had helped his father dig up the potatoes for the last two harvests. The night before they started digging, the potato plants had all been fine and green and a soft, gentle rain had cleared the air. Overnight their food for the whole year had rotted and the fields were a black, stinking mess. The potato blight had poisoned everything.

'I can get a job,' Eamonn's father announced as they trudged along the canal towpath. 'Just as soon as we get to Dublin. I've a strong pair of arms and a broad back. There's plenty a one in Dublin needs a good worker like me.'

'And I can go helping in someone's house,' Eamonn's

mother kept butting in, whenever Daddy gave her the chance to say anything at all. 'The English people have dirty great big houses in Dublin and they do say they need fleets of servants to clean and scrub floors for them and do the cooking an' all. They'd pay money for that too, wouldn't they?'

Eamonn's father laughed. 'And how would you know all that about the big houses in Dublin?' he asked. 'I never knew you'd been to Dublin before I met you.'

'When were you ever there, if it comes to that, you big softhead?' Grandma grumbled. 'It's not only men as can tell stories, you know. Even the little ones have heard of what goes on in Dublin. Everyone knows there's work there, and money to buy things too, for those who aren't afraid of hard work.'

'And we're none of us afraid of work.' Eamonn's mother always walked a little bit faster when she started talking. The canal towpath was narrow and it was hard to keep up with her. 'Grandma can do some sewing for the rich people. There's no one can sew such tiny, neat stitches as Grandma. Shaun, will you watch out that you don't fall into that water?'

Shaun was rather more interested in watching out for things to eat by the side of the canal. If he was lucky, he might find a few dried-up blackberries from last autumn, or even a mushroom. But the birds had usually beaten him to it. Only the yarns they were spinning about life in Dublin helped him to forget he was hungry.

'Will they even give you money for sewing, Grandma?' he asked, walking backwards and perilously close to the water so that he could see her. It was hard to believe that people would pay for something that Grandma did all the time without getting paid.

'Grandma will get more money with her sewing than all of us,' said his father. 'There's that many fine ladies want someone who does tiny stitches to make them beautiful dresses, Grandma won't have a minute to herself. And she'll have that much money she'll open a fine shop and then she'll be far too grand to talk to us any more.'

Grandma laughed, 'Get away with you, you old softhead.'

'And I'll tell you another thing,' Eamonn's father said, not taking any notice of Grandma. 'We won't be living in a cabin any longer. Not in Dublin. In Dublin they have real houses, made of brick, like Mrs Gerrard's house. Only in Dublin it's not just the rich people who live in those sort of houses. There's enough brick houses for all the people to have one of their own. When you look at it like that, Mrs Gerrard did us a favour, turning us out of our cabin. Otherwise we might never have thought of going to Dublin to make our fortune.'

Shaun wrinkled up his nose and looked at his father as if he'd gone loony. Mrs Gerrard hadn't done him any favours, making him sleep out in the open, with only Grandma's shawl to keep him warm. Still, it wouldn't be bad to live in a brick house. He thought maybe the floors would be a bit hard for sleeping on, and he wondered where they would put the turf fire. Then he thought about the pigs they had kept in the years before the potatoes had gone bad. He could almost remember the wonderful taste of bacon with potatoes. There were never any pigs up near Mrs Gerrard's house. Where did the people keep their pigs in Dublin, if they all had posh houses made of brick?

Eamonn didn't believe half of what his father said, but he wished he could believe it. It was nice to have dreams like that. He wondered whether he'd be able to earn money too.

A pair of ducks rose up from the water, quacking and squawking at each other, and flew off into the woods. If he could earn some money, the whole family could go away somewhere. The very best thing would be to get away from Ireland altogether. Eamonn didn't really believe there was a place for them in Dublin because he had stopped believing there was any place in Ireland for people who were poor like them.

It was then that he had his idea, an idea so simple that he couldn't understand why his father hadn't suggested it.

Eamonn suddenly realized that there was a way to save his family. He could move them to a place where they wouldn't have to wander for days looking for somewhere to live. Mr Nolan had told him of a country where there were no poor people because everyone had the same chance of getting a piece of land and working it. There, the potatoes didn't go rotten with disease and the children didn't go round with pains in their stomach from the great big hole where the food should be.

Suddenly, Eamonn was just as desperate as his father to get a job and earn some money. If he could earn money, he could save them. It didn't matter how much money his father earned. Eamonn wanted to earn money as well, because it was his idea; he was going to be the one to take them away from the English soldiers and the landlords and the hunger and everything else that blighted Ireland.

'Are you hungry?' His mother was worried when Eamonn dropped behind the rest and walked along so quietly. She thought she ought to cheer him up so that he would keep on walking. After all their talk, she was convinced that if only she could keep the family going till they got to Dublin they would be able to find enough to eat and everything would be all right again.

Eamonn certainly didn't look downhearted. He was able to forget his hunger and the cold as long as he could hug his wonderful secret, like a hot-water bottle, to his heart. 'Can boys like me earn money too in Dublin?' he asked.

'Ach, you won't be needing to. You can go to school

every day.' His mother's blue eyes shone with excitement. 'Grandma can look after the little ones while she does her sewing and you and Dermot can go to school. A good school. Your Daddy'll be earning money to buy all the things we need. And I'll get money too, and we'll buy you all the books you need for school and even some you don't need. You'll never be a great man if you don't go to school.'

Eamonn liked school, but if there was money to be earned, school could wait. There would be time enough for school when they got away from Ireland.

He smiled back at his mother, but he didn't say anything about his plans. She didn't look weary any longer; she even looked pretty now that she was looking forward to Dublin. Eamonn was determined to work and earn money for her. But he wanted to keep his secret until he had saved up enough money to take them all away. He wouldn't tell them until he had the money. He couldn't wait to see their faces.

On the third freezing cold day after the soldiers had tumbled their house and driven them out of Ballinglas, they came to what looked like an old church, with broken-down walls and an icy blue March sky where the roof had been. All around the church there were the ruins of smaller rooms where only a few stones remained to show that anyone had ever lived there.

'Look, they've even tumbled the churches round here.' Eamonn's father stood in the ruins, where the altar must once have been. 'They didn't let God hang around too long when the landlord decided he'd get more money if he grazed his sheep here.'

'Ach, they didn't do this yesterday,' Grandma said. 'Nor even last year.' She sat down to rest on a huge headstone with a piece of carving like the waves of the sea on the edge of it. 'It takes stronger men than the ones who came to Ballinglas to knock down a monastery. This place must have been done away with hundreds and hundreds of years ago, it looks like. Probably Oliver Cromwell that done it.'

She started to cough and had to lean over to the floor, the way the cough shook her thin body. Eamonn patted her on the back. Grandma was so small and skinny. It was no wonder she got a cough, with the wind howling around them at night, like it had done the night before when they'd had nowhere to sleep but a ditch with some hunks of turf dragged over the top to cover them. The whole night Eamonn had hovered between sleeping and waking, trying to cuddle up to Grandma for warmth. And as long as he had been awake, Grandma had been coughing.

He could tell even his father was having to try extra hard to keep cheerful, to stop the little ones from crying. 'We can rest here tonight,' he said. He picked Eamonn's mother up and whirled her on to the altar stone. 'A bedroom fit for the princess of Dublin,' he cried. Then he lifted Shaun up, and Dermot, 'And all my little princes as well!'

He held out his arms to Eamonn, but Eamonn thought he was too big for that sort of play-acting. 'Ah, go on, Daddy,' he laughed.

'How can we keep the baby warm?' Eamonn's mother was so sad and freezing cold that for once she couldn't join in Daddy's efforts to cheer them all up. 'What can we do to make sure she doesn't freeze? And Mammy?'

Grandma was sitting quietly on the stone where she had flopped herself down when they first got to the old, ruined monastery. It wasn't like her to be so quiet as long as Daddy was in the mood for play-acting. Usually she was the one making jokes and telling everyone not to go round with a face as long as the River Shannon. She looked wearily at Eamonn and her eyes filled with tears.

'Perhaps you can find some turf to make a fire,' she

whispered. She couldn't talk any louder; the coughing had taken her voice away. Then she smiled, 'It was all for the best that the soldiers took old Mr Galvin off to the poorhouse. He wouldn't have been able to walk as far as we've had to, bless him. He'll have a nice warm bed now. And stirabout to eat. In the poorhouse, they give them something to eat every day. They never have to feel hungry.'

Grandma acted as if she was talking to someone else or as if she didn't know what she was saying. She had forgotten their agreement not to talk about food until they found something to eat again. She kept on talking to herself even when they were all busy looking for food and no one was listening to her.

There was a spring running all along one side of the monastery. 'I knew we'd find water here.' Eamonn's father was triumphant. 'They always built these monasteries near the best streams. They weren't stupid, those old monks.'

He had found some nettles as well, growing in the ruins, and he put them in the pot with some water while Eamonn's mother was feeding the baby. 'Wasn't Dermot the clever one, hiding that cooking pot under his jacket?' she said. 'We'd all have been starving without our Dermot.'

Eamonn wished he had thought of getting the cooking pot instead of his father's books. Dermot shrugged his shoulders. 'The big one would have been better,' he said, 'but I couldn't have hid that so well.' They had to boil up the little cooking pot three times before everyone had had something hot to eat.

The nettles were bitter and they didn't fill you up, but Eamonn wasn't used to eating a full meal any longer and at least he could warm his hands near the fire.

Eamonn was glad when Shaun fell asleep on his knee beside the fire. It kept him warm, and he didn't care if he didn't manage to go to sleep himself. It was less torture not to sleep at all than to be woken up by the cold every time he had just dropped off to sleep.

He stroked Shaun's curly hair and listened to his father talking again about all the good things they would have to eat and the warm house they would live in just as soon as they got to Dublin and found work. Daddy didn't want to sleep either.

Sometimes Eamonn put his hand in his right trouser pocket and fingered the gold coin that the soldier had given him. If there really were shops in Dublin, places where you could just walk in and buy food, he could buy them all something to eat even before his father found a job. They could have a real feast the minute they arrived in Dublin.

At other times, when he put his hand in his pocket, shifting the weight of Shaun's little body ever so slightly so he could reach inside, Eamonn thought of his secret. If he had money, wasn't it better to save it? It was going to cost an awful lot of money to get the whole family on a ship and away from Ireland. A king's ransom.

Eamonn watched the fire and wondered what sort of jobs there were for boys of his age. He could always pretend he was older if that meant earning more money. He was taller than most boys of his age. He would work night and day if he had to.

The cold and hunger kept him from sleeping that night, that and Grandma coughing so hard that Mammy had to keep going to her and hugging her tight. Daddy sometimes snored as if he had dozed off for a while and sometimes he got up to fetch more turf for the fire. Eamonn longed for the morning to come.

4

Tullamore

Eamonn had never seen a town like Tullamore, with real shops and a doctor's surgery, with factories and a huge, new, sparkling white church. 'Church of Ireland,' his father said, as they passed it on the road, so they didn't think they ought to stop and say a prayer. The only church Eamonn had ever seen before was the white-washed hut down the road from Ballinglas that the villagers had spent a whole weekend building and painting when they first heard the news that a Catholic priest was coming to live there. The Church of Ireland in Tullamore was built of stone and had a steeple that sparkled like white marble in the winter sunshine. Tullamore must be a very grand place.

The shops were too much of a temptation. Eamonn fingered the soldier's coin in his trousers pocket as they all pressed their noses to the window of a baker's shop in King Street. Everything looked as if it were made of gold; there were different-shaped loaves of bread with shining golden crusts, and the madeira cakes were the kind of rich yellow that comes from lots of butter and eggs. There were fancy cakes too, studded with the jewels of ruby red glacé cherries and emerald green angelica.

The window began to cloud over with their hot breath as they pressed their noses against the pane of glass. Eamonn put his hand into his pocket and ran his fingers round the gold sovereign. Then he rushed to the door of the shop and went in. The others all shouted after him, 'Hey, Eamonn! They won't let you in there when we've no money,' but he didn't listen to them.

A young girl about Eamonn's age was in the shop, buying bread for her mother. She couldn't quite reach over the high counter, so the baker's wife leant over to her and handed down two round, brown loaves, thinly wrapped in tissue paper. As the girl put them in her bag, the smell of the freshly baked bread made Eamonn feel faint. He closed his eyes and when he opened them again the girl was gone.

'Well, laddie?' The baker's wife was an egg-shaped lady, not much higher than the high counter herself, with polished black hair plaited tightly round the back of her head and black eyes that sparkled like the currants in a hot cross bun.

Eamonn didn't know the names of any of the things the baker sold, and he couldn't see the bread any more. It was all hidden behind the white curtain that covered the shop window. He wished his mother was with him now, to help him choose, but the baker's wife had spoken in English. He wondered whether all the people were English in Tullamore. It was such a grand place.

He held out his coin. 'I want to buy bread for my Daddy and Mammy and my Grandma and the little ones, Mrs. Is this enough money?' he asked.

The blackcurrant eyes grew large and round as marbles. 'Now where did you find a piece of gold like that, laddie? Someone'll be looking for that money all over the place.'

She looked a little bit frightened, as if she thought Eamonn was going to pull out a big stick and demand all the money she kept in the drawer behind the counter. 'You ought to give it back, you know. Or take it to the policeman, if you've found it on the road. There'll be someone out looking for that money and crying their eyes out.'

She hitched up the straps of her white apron, so that the pie-crust frill of her blouse pressed right up against her double chin.

'I didn't find it, Mrs. Someone gave it to me. A

soldier gave it to me in Ballinglas. Can I buy something with it? Is it enough to buy bread?'

The baker's wife had never heard of a soldier giving away money before. She couldn't possibly believe that Eamonn had come by the money honestly. She pursed her lips and, without saying another word, went into the bakery behind the shop, leaving the door open so that an even stronger smell of freshly-baked bread teased at Eamonn's aching belly. He wanted to go back outside and tell all the others to come in out of the cold. But perhaps the woman wouldn't like them all standing in her shop.

The baker was a man dressed in flour from head to toe. His shiny black shoes, polished every night before he went to bed, had become soft, white snow boots after an hour in the bakery. His fox-red beard was powdered like the tip of a fox's bushy tail.

He came round to Eamonn's side of the counter, through the double wooden door which opened with two bolts. All the time, the blackcurrant eyes peeped over at Eamonn from the other side of the counter, where the baker's wife considered herself a little bit safer.

'He's awful thin,' she said. Now that the baker was there she had stopped being so frightened of Eamonn and her voice was gentler.

'That's what they all look like, the ones that come from Galway,' said her husband. 'Nothing to eat. I don't suppose you've had anything to eat in a day or two, have you, laddie?'

Eamonn shook his head. It was months since he'd had enough to fill his belly. It must have been August the summer before when they had eaten so many potatoes, with fresh buttermilk, that Eamonn had felt his stomach was going to burst. Daddy had said they ought to eat some of them as long as they were good. And he'd been right.

The very next day, the day after their big feast, the

blight had got to their potatoes too. All the potatoes they had stored away had turned black and rotten. Even the second crop of fresh, green plants, with their pretty white flowers which had to die back before you could start to dig the potatoes, were stinking and rotten in the fields. Since then, they'd had a few good meals. They had to kill the pig when there was nothing left to feed her and then they had sent the cow off to be slaughtered to pay the rent. But after that there was nothing, nothing except the food they could find in the hedges.

The baker's wife reached over the counter and held out a currant cake. 'Here, you can have this to keep the wolf from the door,' she said. 'You don't have to pay. Keep your money for when you really need it. That money'll pay a year's rent!'

Eamonn looked at the cake and grinned. Everything was all right again. 'I have to buy something for all my family, Mrs,' he said. 'They're outside and Grandma's coughing. Can you hear my Grandma?'

It was hard not to hear Grandma coughing, even with the unaccustomed noise and bustle of a town like Tullamore. The baker ran outside and made them all come into the shop.

'O, the poor creatures! I'll make them a cup of tea. They're half-starved, Paddy.' The baker's wife ran to the back of the shop again.

'Have you nowhere to live?' she asked, when she had them all sitting down on her shop floor and eating her whole day's supply of currant buns. Eamonn's father didn't want her to feel too sorry for them after she had been so good and given them things to eat. He tried to think of something cheerful to say.

'He says we'll be better off as soon as it's spring,' Eamonn translated. 'He wants to get a job in Dublin and then we'll have a real house to live in.'

'But you can't drag the old lady off all the way to Dublin,' the baker said, bringing a chair from the back of the shop for Grandma. 'Not with the state she's in.'

As if to prove him right, Grandma started to cough again. But she didn't say anything. Eamonn wasn't used to Grandma being so quiet. Perhaps it was because she felt uncomfortable while they were speaking English. Or perhaps the baker was right. Perhaps Grandma was really ill.

'Is there any work here for an able-bodied man?' Eamonn's father wanted to know.

The baker was much taller than his wife. He was broad shouldered and round-bellied as well. He used to say his huge shoulders were the tools of his trade and the belly was his reward. He looked at Eamonn's father who was tall, but as thin as one of the birch trees by the canal. Through his thin jacket, his shoulder-bones stood out like coat hangers.

The baker wondered whether Eamonn's father would be able to lift even one of the bags of flour he had to move from the store-room to the bakery every day. Then he remembered the works the Government had set up to give the starving people a chance to earn their bread. There were more and more hungry people arriving in the towns every week, looking for food and work.

'Tell your dad he ought to try the public works,' he said. 'They have men working there so they can get government wages to feed their families. On that bit of canal outside town, they're shoring up the banks. It's hard work, though. He'll have to go out there and ask them if they're taking anyone else on.'

Grandma couldn't walk any more. It wasn't like her to complain and she didn't. She just stopped in the middle of the road when they were on their way out to the works, and said, 'You'll have to leave me. Maybe I can walk back to the poorhouse when I get my breath back. There'll be a poorhouse in Tullamore, won't there?'

The woman at the poorhouse wasn't going to let

Grandma in when they first got there. She couldn't speak Irish, so Eamonn had to tell her how bad his Grandma felt.

'She hasn't got the fever, has she?' the matron asked sharply. 'This isn't a fever hospital, you know. If it's a fever case you'll have to take her to Dublin. That's where they look after fever. If we took in fever cases here, we'd have the whole town down with it in no time.'

'She's got a bad cough,' Eamonn said. He didn't see why he had to explain that. Anyone could see how bad his Grandma felt. The baker had seen it right away. And the matron could hear how bad her cough was, all the time Grandma was forced to stand there waiting for them to give her a place to rest.

'We walked all the way from Galway and we had nowhere to sleep,' said Eamonn. 'It was too cold for Grandma.'

The matron looked very suspicious. 'I'm already full as it is,' she said, 'and she can't be all that bad if she was strong enough to walk from Galway. You're a tough old bird, aren't you?' she shouted, as if Grandma was deaf and shouting would help her to understand the foreign language the matron was using.

'You know the rules of the workhouse,' she said. Eamonn didn't. He had never been near a workhouse before, because they'd always had enough to eat and a roof over their heads until now. They'd never thought they were poor. Eamonn's father had always paid the rent on time even when the potatoes failed. Eamonn couldn't see why he had to stand there begging this stupid woman to take his Grandma in for the night – except that he felt he had to try to be polite to the woman. The way the baker had spoken had made him suddenly scared that his Grandma might die if she didn't sleep somewhere warm that night.

'The rule is,' continued the matron, 'that I can only take people in if they're destitute and have no one else to support them. Now as far as I can see, your Grandma here obviously has you to support her. How much money have you got?'

Eamonn lied. 'I've never had any money, Mrs.'

'Well, that's a start,' she said, eyeing him suspiciously, 'if you don't have any money you just might be destitute. But I couldn't take the lot of you.'

She pointed to Eamonn's father and mother waiting patiently with the three children. 'That would mean two women's beds and . . . ' Then she gestured at Dermot with an accusing finger. 'Is that a boy or a girl?'

'That's my brother, Dermot.'

'Well, he'd have to get his hair cut before we'd take him in. The inspector's very strict about headlice. And that would mean four men's beds. Can't be done. I haven't even got room on the floor for any more men.'

'My Daddy's sure he's going to get a job tomorrow, on the works,' Eamonn protested. 'It'll only be for a night or two.'

The poorhouse was dangerously low down on food and there was no money to buy any more. The matron didn't welcome the prospect of six more penniless inmates from Galway. She had enough on her mind, thinking how she was going to get the people in Dublin to send her some more food when they just kept on telling her there was no more food.

'Well, you know that once you get some money you can't keep the old woman here,' the matron grunted. She hated these arguments out in the front office as much as the poor people did who were looking for a bed for the night. She wanted to go back into her own warm parlour and carry on drinking her tea, and she had letters to write to Dublin.

'We won't have to,' smiled Eamonn. 'As soon as Daddy has a job we'll find somewhere to live, and then she can come and live with us.'

When the matron got up to take Grandma to the women's dormitory, Eamonn and his mother started to follow her. 'Only inmates allowed into the dormitories,' the matron said. 'We don't want any of the inmates to catch the fever from strangers. You can come and collect her tomorrow.'

5

Kate

There wasn't a soul in Tullamore who believed that Kate Burke's father had just suddenly disappeared like that because he was dead. No one had seen him go and it didn't look as if he had taken any money or clothes with him, but he wasn't the sort that died young.

The old ladies of Tullamore, who were all in love with him, used to say he had the luck of the little people; nothing bad would ever happen to a darling, good-looking man like him. And he wasn't the sort to kill himself either. He was always smiling, with a smile that would brighten your day like sunshine. So when he disappeared it was a mystery that gave people something to talk about for months on end, and then people shrugged their shoulders and said he must have gone off somewhere to have an adventure. They were sure he'd turn up again one day.

Daddy's sister, Aunt Julia, used to tell Kate the story of her great uncle who was a carpenter. One day he had picked up his tool kit and his Bible and headed off for England without so much as a word to anyone. 'He came back to us in the end,' she used to chuckle, patting one of Kate's hands. 'And your Daddy'll turn up one day too. Just when no one's expecting him.' And she laughed as she told Kate for the hundredth time how her great uncle had walked into his wife's kitchen one morning after he'd been away for five years and said, 'I don't want me egg too soft today. You know I can't stand soft boiled eggs.'

But all the gossipers in Tullamore weren't much help to Kate's stepmother. She'd only been married a year when her husband disappeared, so the company he'd worked for wouldn't let her stay in their house. Kate and her two brothers had to move from the lovely big house right in the centre of town next to the whiskey distillery, to the quiet old farmhouse outside Tullamore where her stepmother's father lived. Kate hardly knew the old man when she moved there. He frightened her and she was determined to dislike him just as much as she felt it was her duty to dislike her stepmother.

It was one of Kate's jobs to collect the letters from the post office in town. The postmistress had started refusing to go all the way out to Rickardstown House where they lived because of the number of poor, starving people who were roaming the country lanes searching for something to eat. Miss Doyle seemed to be convinced that they were so hungry they would eat her if they caught her on her own somewhere.

But Kate wasn't afraid, and Granddad reassured her stepmother that it was safe for the children to go out on their own. 'Those poor starving creatures wouldn't hurt a fly,' he used to say. 'They may have stolen the odd bit of food round about, but you never hear of anyone getting hurt.'

So Kate, because she was the eldest in her family, went alone to the post office every Saturday. Sometimes Peter wanted to go with her, but Kate had her own reasons for going to the post office alone. She had a secret to keep.

Every Saturday, as soon as the postmistress gave her the letters, she checked through them to see if there was one from America. If there was, she didn't go straight home but walked off down the road by the canal to read her secret letter. She always hid it carefully in her bodice when she reached the loneliest stretch of road on her way home. More than once, Kate had wondered whether she should tell her stepmother about the letters from America, but usually she decided it would do more harm than good. So she kept quiet.

A boy was standing with his back to her, so close to the canal that it looked as if he might be about to throw himself in. One of the paupers. At least, Kate thought it must be a boy, since he was wearing trousers. They had holes where the knees should be and were far too short for him, held up by a piece of string. But his hair was long and curly like a little girl's. His wild black curls looked as if they had been twisted round with brambles from a hedge, leaving the thorns and bits of dead leaves still tangled up in his hair. He turned round and looked at her.

Horror snatched Kate's breath away and she put her hands up to her throat as if someone were choking her. The face in front of her was a ghost's face, thin and white, with blue and black shadows under the eyes. A sudden instinct told her it was best to try hard not to show she was frightened. People used to say that if you saw a ghost or a mad dog they would leave you alone if you kept calm. The boy looked so terrible that she wanted to scream.

His eyes were far too big for the face they gazed out of so sadly, a face that was thin and sunken in like a very old man's. The arms poking out of his too short sleeves were all bone with only a veil of skin. A skeleton must look the same as his arms.

Kate wanted to put her hand up to cover her eyes. She wanted to cry out for help, or to run away. But she couldn't move and the boy didn't move. He wasn't going to do anything to her. He just stood and looked at her, then turned and stared at the canal, and then looked back at her.

Kate realized she might have got away in those moments when he was looking at the canal, but something held her there. He didn't look as if he wanted to hurt her. She calmed down as she remembered her grandfather's words back at the farm, 'Those poor starving creatures never hurt a fly. They may have stolen the odd bit to eat here and there.' Kate wished she had something to give the boy. Perhaps she could take him home and give him some of her dinner.

But there were thousands of paupers wandering the roads, looking for something to eat, more than ever now, since the potatoes had failed. She wasn't sure Granddad would want her to take the boy home and give him some food. He kept on saying that if they started to give food to one they'd have the whole lot on their hands. Everyone said that feeding the poor was the Government's responsibility. Kate remembered that poor people were supposed to get something to eat in the workhouse and she wondered whether the boy knew that he could ask for food at Tullamore workhouse. It didn't look like it. He didn't look as if he'd had anything to eat for weeks.

She finally plucked up courage to talk to him. 'Are you looking for the workhouse?'

The big eyes stared at her, sad and puzzled. 'I know where the workhouse is, Miss. It's where my grandma died. I'm looking for somewhere to work, Miss, so all the others don't die too. They stopped the works over by the canal four weeks ago, so our Daddy hasn't been bringing home any more money. And we can't find anything more to eat.'

There were always gangs of men digging away at the canal where it left town and headed for Dublin. Kate and her brothers had been forbidden to go near the works because Aunt Julia had warned her stepmother about it. She said you never knew what might happen, with all those big, wild men around with their great, sharp shovels.

'Have they finished the digging over there?' Kate asked.

'The work's not finished, but they won't give them any more money for it.' The boy's voice was soft and quiet. He spoke slowly, as if he was afraid to run out of breath.

'They say no one needs work because it's soon going

to be spring and time for the early potatoes to be harvested again. But we haven't got any potatoes, Miss. We haven't got any land to grow them on.' He was grim and determined. 'So that's why I have to find work.'

'How old are you?' His face looked older and much more wrinkled than Granddad's, but he was only a few inches taller than Kate.

'Have you got a job, Miss? You can tell them I'm fourteen. I work harder than most grown men.' He smiled and the smile looked out of place on the old, thin face. 'But I'm eleven really.' He was the same age as Kate.

'Do you feel strong enough to walk a long way?' she asked.

''Course I'm strong enough to walk a long way! You should have seen how far we walked when we got turned out of our village. Hey! Are you English?'

They had turned away from the canal and begun to walk through the town in the direction of Rickards-town House.

Heads turned at the sight of Kate Burke with one of the paupers, and more than one old lady decided to speak to her stepmother about it.

'That's a crackpot question!' said Kate. 'Now why should I be English?'

'You speak like the English.'

'Ooh, that's a lie. I do not.'

'You do too.'

'Well anyway, you've got a queer accent yourself.'

Somehow it didn't feel quite right that a boy whom Kate was intending to feed and give some decent clothes to should be arguing with her like that. He ought to be grateful that she was talking to him. He grinned at her, 'What's your name?'

'My name's Kate Burke and my father used to be manager at the whiskey distillery, but he's not here any more. We live with my stepmother's family.'

Eamonn could sense that she didn't think much of

that arrangement, so he didn't ask anything more about where she lived.

'What did your daddy die of?'

Kate felt she was entitled to her secrets as much as anyone.

'Do you always go round poking your nose into other people's business?'

Eamonn shrugged his shoulders and they walked on in silence. He could walk quite quickly for someone who looked so ill.

Rickardstown House was at the end of a long driveway lined with rose bushes, with stately yew trees standing guard behind them. Nobody dared to go near Rickardstown House unless they were invited.

'Wait here,' Kate said when they had managed to creep, unseen, round to the back of the house. 'I can get you something to eat if no one's in the kitchen.'

'I've got two little brothers and a baby sister as well,' Eamonn whispered as she slipped across the yard and in at the back door.

Eamonn went and hid inside the dark barn. As soon as he got used to the gloom, he started to walk slowly along by the cow stalls, counting the animals. He had never seen so many pigs and cows before. Back in Ballinglas you might have seen the odd one. In good times, all except the poorest families had had an old pig to fatten up or a cow to give them milk. Someone who was a little bit richer might have had a donkey.

Eamonn lost count when he got to twenty cows, all down one side of the barn, and there were more along the other wall. The pigs, eight of them, each in their own separate pen, were at the far end of the barn. Eamonn inspected them, giving low whistles at each new wonder, as he saw how many of the sows had farrowed, each of them suckling four or five tiny, wriggling piglets. After he had finished staring at the pigs, he realized that the barn went much further along than he had at first thought. Through a small half-door, there was a huge, high section where all the farm machines were kept and where the roof soared up as high as a church to make a loft for the hay.

Kate couldn't find him when she came back into the barn and she didn't want to make any noise because she still wasn't sure what her grandfather would have to say about her feeding paupers. She jumped when Eamonn came upon her suddenly, out of the darkness near the pigsties.

'Why do you keep them all inside when the weather's so grand? Whoever heard of pigs and cows indoors at the end of April?'

'Granddaddy says its best to feed them the grass in here, so they don't trample it all down. And my Aunt Julia says they would all get stolen if we left them out in the fields.' Kate was ashamed to admit that was the reason for keeping the animals inside. 'There's so many people with nothing to eat.' She didn't like to look at him after she'd said that. 'My stepmother's in the kitchen. She says you're to come and get something to eat, but you're to make sure you wipe your feet.'

Kate was surprised. Her stepmother had come into the kitchen and caught her just when she was cutting some bread for Eamonn. But she had smiled and said that it was right for Kate to give the boy something to eat. Kate never liked to ask her stepmother for favours in case that was taken as a sign that she had grown to like her. But she hadn't had to ask this time. It was her stepmother who said they couldn't just send the boy away with nothing to eat after he had walked all the way to their house.

While Eamonn was eating in the kitchen, Kate's stepmother kept one ear on the door to the parlour, where Granddaddy was sleeping. She knew her father wouldn't have stopped her feeding the starving boy. He would probably have been very nice to Eamonn if he had walked into the kitchen and found him tucking into beef and carrots left over from the lunchtime stew. But she knew that afterwards he would have grumbled and said they couldn't afford to start feeding the paupers because if you fed one you'd have the whole lot on your hands. And then he would have complained again about Kate's father running off and leaving him to feed and clothe all those extra children. She didn't want to give him any more reasons to complain. Luckily, Granddaddy didn't wake up.

When Eamonn went home they weighed him down with bags of bread and cheese and apples, enough to feed the whole family for a week. And Kate and her stepmother kept on feeding Eamonn and his family, secretly, without telling Granddaddy, for six weeks. Then the Government sent more money for the workers, the canal work started all over again, and Eamonn stopped coming. Kate missed him. She looked for him every time she was down in Tullamore, but he seemed to have just disappeared into thin air.

6

Hunger

Daddy refused to change his mind. It was because he wasn't used to being poor. He didn't like other people helping him. Back in their village in Galway, he had always been the man other people came to for help. If the schoolteacher was busy, people would ask Eamonn's father to read letters for them. If they had a load to carry from far away he would lend them the donkey for a day or two. Strangers who had no house of their own and were forced to wander the roads had always been sure of a bed for the night if they knocked at the door of Eamonn's cabin. Eamonn didn't know what it was like to be rich, but he had never thought of himself as poor.

Eamonn had not been to visit Kate and her stepmother out at the farm for more than four weeks. It wasn't that he didn't want to, nor that he didn't have time. There would have been plenty of time to go when he wasn't out looking for food.

But as soon as Eamonn's father had got work again down by the canal, he had forbidden the children to go out begging for food. He thought he should be able to support his family and keep them well-fed and he felt ashamed whenever he had to ask for help. Eamonn couldn't understand it. Kate's stepmother had done so much for the family but Daddy told Eamonn he mustn't go near her. He said that if Eamonn went up to the house she would still feel she had to give him food for the family, and that wouldn't be right now that he had work and they were able to feed themselves.

Daddy promised Eamonn that he could go and see Kate just as soon as they had enough money to buy a little present for Kate's stepmother, or perhaps pay her back by helping with the harvest. But he wouldn't hear of the children going to visit Rickardstown House until harvest time. It was no use Eamonn protesting that he could go and see Kate's stepmother and tell her they didn't need any more help. His father just shook his head and said that they had to stand on their own two feet.

Eamonn missed Kate. She was the only real friend he had made in Tullamore and now that he couldn't even go to school, he needed friends.

He spent his days out with Dermot looking for any wild plants they could eat. His father was paid every evening and brought home enough money for one meal a day, but still the boys were always hungry. They chewed on dandelion leaves to fool their stomachs into thinking they were getting a good meal, and took nettles home for their mother to make into soup. If they were lucky, a shopkeeper might give them an apple for doing an odd job for him, but every week there were fewer shopkeepers and more hungry boys out looking for scraps to eat. A boy they met near the poorhouse told them he once found a whole loaf of bread on top of someone's pile of rubbish. 'There was only a bit of mould on it,' he grinned. 'You wouldn't believe the things people throw out. I had to rub the dirt off a bit, of course.'

After that, Dermot and Eamonn searched all the rubbish heaps every day, but they never found anything to eat there. 'We were daft to believe that boy,' Dermot said. 'No one would ever throw food away.'

One night, less than two weeks after the canal-works had been restarted, Dermot and Eamonn made their way home. They had been out all day and hadn't found a single bit of food; nobody had had any odd jobs for them to do either. It was after seven o'clock and they sat with Mammy and the two little ones in the dark room they had rented with the soldier's gold sovereign. 'Your Daddy'll be home in two shakes of a lamb's tail,' Mammy said to Shaun, 'and then we'll all go out and have a feast with his wages.'

Even Dermot knew that she was telling lies about the feast. Eamonn had noticed how his mother hardly ate anything at night time when they had their meal. She kept slipping extra spoonfuls of the coarse cornmeal porridge to Dermot and Shaun, and Eamonn saw how weary and ill she looked when they still said they were hungry. He always shook his head when she tried to give him some of her food.

He was old enough to know what the problem was. His father was getting the same amount of money as he had been getting a few months ago, before they had stopped the works for a time, but the food now cost twice as much. And there were people who had enough money to pay three times as much as the asking price. Eamonn's parents bought less and less food every week, and every week, the price of cornmeal rose even higher.

Rosaleen started to cry and Eamonn's mother nestled the baby up close to her breast and tried to feed her. 'Daddy'll be home in two minutes, Shaun,' she said, reaching one arm round the baby's head and stroking his hair.

It was too dark for Eamonn to see her face, but he thought of how thin his mother had got. The baby was taking everything out of her. Rosaleen had a round, fat little belly, so fat that it looked like a balloon about to burst. She certainly didn't seem to be going hungry, if you didn't pay too much notice to the way her arms and legs were spindle thin.

No one spoke and Eamonn heard the noise of the baby sucking energetically at his mother's breast. Then she pulled her head away impatiently and started crying again.

'She's greedier than all the rest of you put together,'

laughed his mother. 'I'll have to give her some more milk when your father comes home with the food.'

Eamonn knew he could have got milk from Kate's farm. If they could only give the baby cow's milk, his mother wouldn't get so thin and tired. He thought of the cheese Kate's stepmother had given them and his stomach groaned. Perhaps he could go to Kate's grandfather and offer to work in return for a bite to eat.

They heard steps along the long hallway. 'There's your Daddy now.' Eamonn could tell, even in the dark, that his mother was smiling and the baby stopped crying as if she knew that his arrival meant the arrival of more food.

Eamonn went to open the door and Shaun and Dermot catapulted past him, both wanting to be the first to give their father a hug. Usually, Daddy threw them both up into the air, one after the other and joked about them getting heavier every day. But he wasn't in the mood for jokes. He patted them both on the head and touched Eamonn's cheek, 'How are you, laddies?' Then he went over to the window and sat down with his back against the wall. It was a long time before he spoke.

'I didn't get my money today,' he said. 'There was no one there to pay out the wages.'

Eamonn's mother sighed. 'If it's no worse than that we'll manage,' she said. 'We can manage until to-morrow.'

No one came to pay the wages the next day, or the next. None of the men had been paid for a whole week, and still the money didn't come. Every day the man in charge of the works said they would definitely get their money the very next day and after ten days it still hadn't come. None of the men wanted to make trouble in case they were thrown off the works for good. If they were thrown off the works they couldn't buy any food at all for their families, so they kept quiet and went along to work every day.

Eamonn and Dermot did what they could to find food. Once, Eamonn asked his father whether he could go out to Kate's farm. 'They'd understand that it's not our fault we haven't got anything to eat,' he pleaded. 'It's not because you haven't been working.'

But his father shook his head. 'I won't have children of mine going out begging,' he said. 'The money should be here tomorrow.'

Eamonn's mother grew more and more tired. They got a very small ration of soup or cornmeal from the poorhouse, but she gave most of hers away to the children. 'I'm not hungry,' she said. She seemed to be almost too tired to eat.

Then a man from the works told Eamonn's father that they had opened a government food depot in a town about thirty miles away from Tullamore. They were giving food away free to anyone who needed it. Daddy decided to walk there with the man. 'I may be away longer,' he said. 'If there's work there, paying work, I'll stay there till I can come home with money as well as the free food.'

Eamonn wanted to go with him. He told his father that the two of them could bring back twice as much grain, or whatever it was they were giving away, but Daddy said it was better if he stayed at home. Someone had to go over to the works every day to try and collect his wages for the last two weeks. And as soon as Eamonn got the money he could go out and buy them all something good to eat. 'I need to leave a man in charge while your Mammy doesn't feel so well,' his father said.

Every day during the next two weeks Eamonn went out to the little office near the works to ask for his father's wages and every day the man in the grey tweed suit told him that the money hadn't arrived from the Government yet, but it was bound to come the next day. Whenever he heard that, Eamonn wondered whether he should go and ask Kate's stepmother for help. But he always remembered the promise he had made to his father, and decided to wait just one more day. If the money isn't there tomorrow, he told himself, I'll have to go and beg them to give us some food. And every day he decided to wait just a little longer.

7

The Glasses Man

Kate's stepmother was washing her hair when the glasses man came. It was infuriating. While her stepmother was pouring cold water over her head into the basin, she had to kneel on the hard chair listening to the squeals of excitement down below as the other children rushed out to meet him. The glasses man always did wonderful tricks with lenses, making rainbows for the children and showing them how you could make things look bigger or smaller with his machine like a telescope.

By the time the six months had gone round between one visit and the next, they had always forgotten his tricks and the marvellous stories he had to tell about folks in Dublin. And it wasn't just Dublin that he could talk about; when he did the round of all his regular customers his travels took him right over to the West of Ireland and up as far as the Giant's Causeway. The children especially liked his stories about the giants up there at the tip of Ireland who used to throw stones at each other, just like any brothers and sisters having a pillow fight. He told stories from foreign countries as well, and the stories sounded much more exotic than when Kate's stepmother read them aloud from the big fairy tale book, because of his funny German accent.

Kate wriggled and squirmed, like a cat that's decided it doesn't want to be stroked any longer.

'Child!' her stepmother groaned, 'will you hold still while I give these rats' tails a rinse out.' She yanked at Kate's long brown hair, trying to rinse it out with more freezing cold water, and Kate let out a squeal of pain. 'Ach, you've a terrible head of hair on you, child. Nothing but rats' tails. I can't have you going downstairs with all this soap in it. Otherwise we won't get the tangles out till next week. And you won't like that. Don't squeal so much, child! Anyone would think I was murdering you.'

Kate struggled again. 'But I want to see the glasses man.'

'He'll be there when we get down,' her stepmother said. 'I told your Granddaddy that I want him to leave a pair for me, so there's no hurry.'

Kate didn't like to hear her stepmother say 'your Granddaddy'. 'He isn't mine!' she wanted to protest. 'He's Joe's Granddaddy, but he isn't mine. My Grand-daddy is in Tullamore in the graveyard and he was nice to me. I never had to keep quiet when he came to visit in our house. My real Granddaddy never shouted at me.'

Kate squealed again as she felt more tugs at her wet, tangled hair. She couldn't help thinking of her real mother whenever she felt bad about something. She often liked to think of her. Mammy shouldn't have died like that, just a week after Peter was born. And it wasn't right that Kate's daddy had married again so fast. He had never even asked her what she thought of having someone else to take her mother's place. He had just taken Kate on his knee the night before the wedding and said, 'I'm only doing it for you, my Katie, so's you can have a real mammy again.'

Kate's real mother used to say nice things about her hair. 'It's like silk!' she would say to Daddy, whenever Kate was all dressed up for a party, with her hair brushed a hundred times to make it shine. 'It's worth all the untangling it takes to see it shine like that. She makes me think of the story of Rapunzel or Rumpel-stiltzkin when I've brushed her hair to shining gold.' Daddy liked Kate to wear her hair loose as well, cascading down her back and tied with a satin ribbon. But her stepmother said she didn't look like a lady unless she had her hair braided tightly and pinned close to her head.

By the time Kate went downstairs, Mr Stein's glasses were all spread out on a green baize cloth on the kitchen table, and he sat in Granddaddy's armchair at the head of the table polishing them, while Granddaddy and her stepmother tried different pairs on and inspected themselves in the large, round mirror the glasses man carried on his back.

Granddaddy had already decided to take the same kind of glasses he always had, with round tortoiseshell frames. The glasses man chuckled. 'I knew you'd choose that pair,' he said, 'I brought them specially for you. You wouldn't believe it, but they're all the rage now, in Dublin. I've been carrying those glasses for the last twenty years, and suddenly they're all the rage.'

He started to polish up his tiny sample pairs of gold-rimmed glasses. He sometimes let the children play with his samples and try them on their dolls, but he wasn't feeling very generous today and let out a long-suffering sigh. 'If you can talk of a rage, the way business is treating me at the moment.'

Kate handed him the cup of tea that her stepmother had made as soon as they came downstairs. She looked closely at his face and wondered why his nose was so long and thin and red. Did his glasses pinch him the way the sample glasses had pinched at her nose when she had tried them on in secret, because they were far too small for her? His cheeks were as pink as carnations and he had fluffy white hair that stood on end as if it was electrified. He let out another sigh that made Kate want to go over and pat him on the shoulder so he would feel better.

'That bad, is it?' Granddaddy looked worried.

'There's no one with the money to buy glasses any more.' Mr Stein shook his head. 'I'm thinking of packing up and going to America. I've got a brother in New York. There's a good living to be made in New York, so he tells me.'

'But aren't there lots of rich people in Dublin as well, Mr . . . ?' Kate's stepmother always forgot the names of the travelling salesmen who only came once or twice a year. 'I should have thought the Dublin people'd be needing glasses too, when they get old.'

The glasses man shook his head. Kate thought he looked like a sad leprechaun. All he needed was a long, red pointed hat to make her believe he was only pretending to be sad so she wouldn't ask him for his pot of gold. 'There aren't no more rich people in Dublin, Mrs,' he said. 'All the ones as could afford to go have gone off to England. Or America. There's nobody lives in Dublin now but poor, homeless starving wretches, all looking for work that no one can give them.'

Kate hadn't seen Eamonn for about a month, ever since his father had got work on the canal again. She knew that Eamonn's father had been planning to move the whole family to Dublin and look for a better job, but it sounded as if Dublin was even worse than Tullamore.

Kate was sad when Eamonn suddenly stopped coming to their house, even though she knew things must be going better for him and his family. She wondered what he was doing. It was hard to believe that Eamonn and his family would go off to Dublin without saying goodbye. Kate was sure they must still be living in the house where she had once visited them. And if the glasses man was right, she should go and warn them not to risk travelling to Dublin.

During the month she hadn't seen Eamonn, Kate had often thought of going to visit him in his house at the other end of Tullamore, but his family were still very poor and she didn't like to go empty-handed. The only thing which prevented her from going was that she still hated the idea of having to beg her stepmother for food. She never wanted to ask her stepmother for anything because then she would be forced to be grateful to her. But Kate was worried that Eamonn and his family might be going short of food. Every night she decided that she would definitely ask her stepmother for help the very next day. And every morning she decided to wait just one more day to see if Eamonn would come to visit them.

The glasses Kate's stepmother chose had a silver frame. 'They're that light you'll hardly notice you're wearing them, Mrs,' said the glasses man.

Peter wanted glasses too, but everyone laughed and said he was too young. 'You wait until you're my age,' Granddaddy said. 'Then you'll wish you didn't have to wear them. I'm always losing the dratted things and when I don't have them on I can't see to find them. Glasses aren't for children.'

The glasses man did a few more tricks before he left but they could tell his heart wasn't in it. 'You'll probably have to send to Dublin for your glasses next year,' he said, carefully packing his samples into their separate compartments in his two leather bags. 'America's the only place to go now, as long as you've still got a bit of money to get you there.'

While all the others were still watching Mr Stein pack, Kate's stepmother leaned over and whispered, 'Don't you want to take a few things over to Eamonn and his Mammy and Daddy? You haven't seen him for such a long time. I've got some food for them in the kitchen.'

It shocked Kate to count the weeks since they had last seen Eamonn. After her first meeting with him by the canal he had come to get food every week, on a Saturday when Granddaddy was out at market. Kate and her stepmother had watched him slowly regaining his health and strength.

Once, Eamonn had taken Kate to visit his family, but

since his father had started work again he hadn't been near them.

Kate helped her stepmother to pack the food in silence. She didn't mention Eamonn's father and his plans to move on to Dublin. He wouldn't have talked of going there to get work and boasted about how much money they could earn when they got there if he had heard what the glasses man had to say. If they hadn't already set off, it was high time Kate went to see them, to tell them what the glasses man had said and warn them not to go.

Granddaddy told the glasses man he would walk on to the next farm with him, so Kate waited until she thought they were well on their way. Then she set off, walking as fast as she could, with Peter beside her carrying an extra basket.

But they had forgotten how fast Granddaddy could walk to the next farm and back. When he saw Kate and Peter going down the lane with the two big baskets of food he stopped them. 'Where are you two heading for?' he smiled. 'A picnic in the woods? Does your mother know you're running away with all this food?'

The only reason Kate had managed to keep her one big secret, about the strange letters she had received from America, was because no one had any idea she was hiding anything. Kate wasn't a very good liar. If anyone had thought to ask her, she would have been forced to tell them all about the American letters and who they came from. So when Granddaddy asked her where she and Peter were going, she had no choice but to tell him who the food in her basket was for. It was obvious they weren't just going on a picnic. She had enough ham and eggs and bread to feed the family for a week.

Peter looked at Granddaddy anxiously, expecting him to start grumbling about all the mouths he already had to feed, but he just said, 'I'd better come with you if they live down there. I don't want you youngsters wandering around on your own. It's not the safest part of town for children.' He quickly went back up the lane to the farm and came back with a pail of milk and some butter from the dairy.

8

The Nightmare

There were hordes of soldiers in Tullamore. The children were used to the sight of British soldiers. It was nothing to see two or three of them strolling around together down near the workhouse or standing outside the town hall, where they gave out tickets for the men who wanted to get work on the roads. But this time it was impossible to count them. There must be hundreds and hundreds of soldiers marching through the narrow streets and there were more of them forcing their way into the town from every direction.

'There's going to be trouble.' Granddaddy frowned. When he was angry about something, deep lines appeared in his forehead and there were dark shadows around his eyes, like the grey clouds that block out the sun before a thunderstorm. 'We'd better take ourselves off home and come back tomorrow to see your friends. This is no place for children.'

He tried to go back the way they had come, but soldiers were coming into town that way as well. They could see that it would be impossible to make their way back until the soldiers had passed. Men, women and crying children, all crushed together, were hurtling towards them because the soldiers and their horses took up all the space in the narrow streets.

Granddaddy pushed Kate and Peter into a side street that led down to the canal. 'We'll go where it's quiet,' he said. There were deep furrows cutting his face between his nose and the corners of his lips. These lines, which only ever appeared when he was extremely angry, made it look as if someone had painted his face with lines of grey war-paint.

The road by the canal was quieter, but still crowded; too many people had followed them down the little side street. They were being thrust closer and closer to the trouble that Granddaddy wanted to avoid.

When they got to the canal, they could go no further. Kate looked beyond the bridge to her left and saw a large group of thin, ragged men standing on the same bank as they were, most of them absolutely silent. She couldn't understand how such a huge crowd could be so quiet, standing there with their bony shoulders hunched and their sad eyes staring at the opposite bank. All she could think of were the tattered, scrawny ravens she saw scanning Granddaddy's empty, ploughed fields in winter, scouring the land for something to eat.

On the other side of the canal soldiers were lined up as far as Kate could see. Every few seconds more soldiers joined them and lined up in rows behind them. The sun flashed on the polished steel of bayonets at the ready. The soldiers in the front row had loaded guns which were pointing at Kate and her brother.

Granddaddy put his arms around the two of them, 'We musn't stay here, Katie,' he said. But then he stayed rooted to the spot like people are supposed to do when they are hypnotized by some poisonous snake and they can't take their eyes off the creature that wants to kill them. One of the poor, ragged men in the crowd to the left of Kate moved slightly. He might have been only brushing the hair out of his eyes or shifting his weight from one foot to the other, but it was enough. The soldiers in the front line suddenly stiffened, fingers on the triggers of their guns.

An officer at the end of the line on his horse raised his sword in the air. The harness jingled as the horse pranced and backed up nervously. The world seemed to hold its breath. The only sounds Kate noticed were the jingling harness and a baby crying. She had time to wonder how badly it would hurt to be shot by one of those huge guns the soldiers were pointing at her. She couldn't run or cry. The world stood still. Then, for some reason, the officer decided not to give the order to fire. He lowered his sword very slowly.

Through the gap made when the man had moved to one side, Kate was soon able to see what was happening on the canal. Twenty scared-looking men were working very quickly, loading the long canal boats with heavy sacks. 'That's wheat,' Granddaddy whispered. But he seemed to be talking to himself rather than to Kate. 'They're sending the wheat away to fatten up England. They're leaving these poor beggars to die.'

By the time Granddaddy managed to make a path for them through the crowds of people, the barges were nearly full.

And still the rows of ragged, starving men stood on the canal bank in silence. And still the soldiers knelt there on the opposite bank, with bayonets fixed, while the reserve troops held their horses in check behind. The people didn't look as if they'd have the strength to walk, let alone fight with soldiers who were armed to the teeth with bayonets and rifles.

'But why are they sending the wheat away, Granddaddy? Mr O'Rourke, the baker, would have bought it off them. He could have stayed in Tullamore if they'd given him some wheat.' Peter had always been Mrs O'Rourke's favourite. She had treated him to a currant bun every time he went to the baker's shop with his stepmother.

As soon as they managed to make their way through the crowd and head away from the canal towards the lane where Eamonn lived, the streets of Tullamore became silent and empty.

Lots of shops had been shut up for good since the potato crops had failed. Mr O'Rourke, the baker who had fed Eamonn's family when they first arrived in Tullamore, had shut up shop at the end of July, and gone to America. It looked as if everyone in Ireland who had the money was going to America.

Granddaddy shrugged his shoulders. 'Mr O'Rourke didn't have enough money to buy their wheat,' he said. 'The prices were too high. And there weren't that many could afford to buy bread from him any more. They're sending the wheat away so they can get more money for it.'

Eamonn had sometimes had nightmares like this, when his mind wanted him to rush forward, to escape from some unseen enemy, but his legs refused to move. He knew that he should be running faster than he had ever run in his life before, but his legs wouldn't do what he wanted them to do. Why did he have to keep stopping to walk? Why couldn't he run as fast as he used to do? He cursed his weak, old man's legs and his thumping heart that made him have to slow down after every twenty steps. There was something wrong with baby Rosaleen and he had to get help.

He had thought of going to the poorhouse but that wouldn't have done any good. They would have asked him why Rosaleen's mother wasn't looking after her, and then he would have lost precious time trying to convince them that his mother was very sick too. He didn't know what was wrong with them all. His mother and Shaun and Dermot just lay in one corner of the room, hardly moving. And the baby had stopped crying.

That was the frightening thing. Until now, she had cried when she was hungry and his mother had fed her, but his mother was too sick to feed the baby. Eamonn had tried to get her to take bits of the dandelion leaves he found, or the cornmeal porridge he queued up for every night from the poorhouse. But those things just made the baby more sick. And now she had stopped crying. She lay quietly next to Eamonn's mother, her quick breathing like the flutterings of the baby sparrows Eamonn used to pick up when they fell out of their nests.

Eamonn broke into a run again. It was all his father's fault because he had told the children not to go begging. As soon as he found work, he had told Eamonn not to keep asking for food at Kate's farm. But the food they could buy with the money from his work was never enough, even in the weeks when the clerks came and paid the men their wages every day. And now the baby was dying. He shouldn't have left her alone.

For a moment Eamonn stopped and almost turned back. Then he remembered that he had had to leave them all alone to go and get help. His mother hadn't been able to tell him what to do. She was so sick that she hardly answered his questions. His father was miles away, with the other men who had heard of a place where they were giving out food. Kate's stepmother was the only person he knew who could help.

The town was so empty and quiet. If he had bumped into someone while he was running along the road Eamonn might have been able to ask them for help. What if Kate's mother wasn't there? He got so worried about leaving the baby all alone that he decided he would ask the very next person he saw on the road to come back with him to the house. There would be time enough then to go for Kate's mother. But there wasn't a soul about. It was like on a Sunday morning when everyone was at church, except that even on a Sunday you could be sure of running into someone who was late.

He ran past the Catholic church, a white shed with a thatched roof on the poor side of the town. If it had been a Sunday there would have been groups of men standing outside gossiping while the women were inside doing their praying.

The streets were so deathly quiet that when Eamonn slowed down to a walking pace, all he could hear was the sound of his own breath coming in great gasps. Why were there no children out on the roads, begging? There wasn't even a soldier near the town hall. A soldier might have been able to help. There were usually crowds of men out on the steps of the town hall, waiting patiently to be let in so they could beg for the ticket they needed to get a job on the works.

Eamonn reached the fork where one road went right towards the canal and the other went left towards Rickardstown House. Then he thought he heard distant shouting. Yes, people were shouting. It sounded as if the whole town was out by the loading bays of the canal, near the warehouses, shouting like they did to cheer on the horse they wanted to win on race days, but it was impossible to make out any of the words they were shouting.

When they all suddenly went silent, Eamonn slowed down to a walk again. He couldn't help himself. He had to find out what was happening. Perhaps some canal boats had arrived and brought more food and the people were cheering because of that. There must be some reason why the whole town was down by the canal.

In the split second while he considered whether he should run down and take a look at what was happening, a single shot ripped open the silence. There was a scream and then a roar from the crowd and then a sudden explosion of shots and more screaming.

Eamonn turned and ran in the direction of Rickardstown House. He didn't know what was happening down by the canal, but whatever it was he knew it wasn't safe for him to hang around. The only thing he could be sure of was that they had brought guns instead of food to the people. Eamonn ran on and on until it felt as if his lungs were bursting and still he didn't seem to be getting any closer to the farmhouse.

He remembered the times he had walked out to the farm with Kate, when the walk had seemed too short because they were chattering and arguing the whole way. It shouldn't be so hard to run to Rickardstown House for a boy who had walked all the way from Galway. His chest ached whenever he tried to go faster and he panicked about what might be happening at home while he was away. He shouldn't have slowed down for so long to see what was happening down by the canal. He blamed himself now because there was no one to look after the baby, but he couldn't have stayed with her and watched her get worse while he did nothing. The shots he had heard coming from the canal rang through his head. He heard the screaming again, though he was already a mile away. Something terrible must have happened down there. Perhaps the English soldiers had killed people.

Eamonn tried to quicken his pace again. Was it any worse if the soldiers did shoot you? Was that worse than dying slowly because you didn't have enough to eat? He was angry. Why should everything go so disastrously wrong again? Why did all the bad things happen to his family? Hadn't they had enough bad luck already? It was about time something good happened. Eamonn had pawned the pullover Kate's stepmother had given him so that he could buy paper and stamps. Then he had written letters to two of his aunts who lived in America. He felt sure that if his relatives knew how bad things were they would send the money to take the whole family to America.

Eamonn had tried to get work on the roads with his father as well, but the overseers wouldn't take him. They said there was only enough money to pay one wage per family. So he had given up all hope of earning enough to buy the tickets for their passage to America and he very soon realized that if he did earn any money he would have to give it to his parents for food. His only hope was that one of his aunts would send them the money for their passage as soon as she got his letter. Eamonn was impatient for the money to come. The

only thing which kept him going was that he was sure it
would come, eventually. People who went to America
always earned a lot of money. It was about time
Eamonn's family had a stroke of good luck.

He reached the driveway to Rickardstown House,
where the rose bushes and the yew trees stood to
attention as if they were awaiting an inspection by
Kate's grandfather. Eamonn wasn't scared of him. He
was past caring whether he met Kate's grandfather or
not. He was meant to be fierce, but surely even a fierce,
grumpy old man wouldn't refuse to help them once
Eamonn told him that his baby sister was dying.

He started to sprint up the drive. He knew he could
manage the last stretch. After Kate's stepmother had
begun to give them food, he had often raced Kate and
her brother all the way up the drive to their back door.
Kate had always beaten him, but he had never had to
stop running and walk part of the way.

Before he saw the house, his chest began to ache and
pains like fire shot over his right shoulder. He had to
stop running again. He was useless. The baby would die
because of him. He started to cry and walked to the
back door. He knocked at the door and then leant
against it, gasping for breath and sobbing. All he could
think of, as he rested, slowly getting his breath back,
was what he would say to Kate's fierce grandfather. 'I
won't come begging ever again,' he was going to say.
'But you've got to help us just this once. Please.'

Kate's stepmother opened the door.

The big, old house where Eamonn lived had been home
to ten families when they first arrived. Eamonn had
paid out the whole of his gold sovereign to the landlord
so they would have somewhere to live for the next year.
Now there were only two families left. No one knew
where the rest had gone. If a family didn't pay the rent
at the end of the year the landlord threw them out on

the streets, but no one knew where they went after that.

Granddaddy went first. Kate never knocked when she went to visit, but he knocked at the old door with its peeling, faded blue paint. Then he stood back to take a look at the house. 'I can still remember when this was a really grand house,' he said. 'It's not so long ago either. An English man used to live here with his family and a great crowd of servants.'

'It's open,' Kate said. 'No one ever knocks.'

The house was quiet. The first time Kate had been to visit, two little boys had been sitting in the dark hall with Eamonn's two younger brothers and there had been noises coming out of every room. Now there was no one around.

They walked along the hallway. It smelt damp and mouldy like some deep, dark cave. Kate felt Granddaddy catching hold of her hand and he took Peter's hand as well. Was he frightened?

She wasn't used to it being so quiet, especially by the time they were outside the room where Eamonn lived. She listened for the sound of the baby crying, or the two little boys fighting, but there was nothing.

Suddenly, Kate was frightened too. She pushed open the door of their room. 'Hello!' she called out. Then she stopped, right in the doorway, with Peter and Granddaddy standing behind her. It was a large room with a high ceiling, where crystal chandeliers had once thrown light on fine dinner parties. Now, in the far corner the light from the broken window showed Eamonn's mother lying on the floor with the three little ones. None of them moved.

Granddaddy rushed across the room. 'God help us.' He sounded hoarse, as if something was caught in his throat. 'The poor wretches are starving.'

Kate and Peter walked slowly over to where Granddaddy was kneeling down beside Eamonn's mother on the floor. Kate felt shy, like she did when she was being forced to meet some strange new friend of her parents.

71

She didn't want to look. She didn't want to believe that there was something wrong. Granddaddy put his hand on the mother's shoulder. Then he gently touched the three children. He rested his hand on the baby's forehead for a long time, and Kate saw that he was crying.

'Bring me the pail of milk, child,' he said. He spoke very gently, as if Kate were the one who was sick and he had to take care not to upset her. But it was too much for him when he turned back again to the baby. He stroked her head gently, as if he was afraid he might wake her. 'The babby's dead,' he said.

Kate touched the poor little thing. She was cold. Kate had seen a dead calf before and she remembered feeling annoyed about the death because its mother hadn't bothered about it very much. She had been sad when her father disappeared and everyone wondered if he was dead or not. But this was different. Kate couldn't understand a baby dying. Rosaleen had been so healthy and round. Even when all the others looked thin and worn out with the hunger she had always looked well-fed. And it couldn't be more than eight weeks since Kate had last been to see them with food from her stepmother. Eamonn had told her they were going to buy food every day with the money his father got from his work.

Granddaddy was trying to dampen Shaun's lips with some of the milk. He was too weak to drink it. 'You must drink some of this, child.' Granddaddy shouted at first and shook the little boy, but then he became quieter and took him on his knee. 'You must drink.'

They heard the outside door banging and then the sound of bare feet running down the long hallway.

'I've been out to your house.' Eamonn was weak and out of breath. He stopped himself from falling by leaning against the wall, supporting himself like an old man. Then he walked slowly round the room to where his mother lay. 'I knew you'd help us. Your Mammy's coming too.'

'But how did it get so bad?' Kate cried. 'Poor little Rosaleen.'

Eamonn leant against the wall and slowly slid down it until he was sitting near the baby. He put his hand out to touch her red-gold curls.

'That's why I came to your house,' he said. 'I knew your Granddad didn't want paupers about the place. But when the baby was so bad and Mammy was sick I didn't know what to do. And your stepmother's been good to us, even when you weren't there. I thought I could bring help before it was too late.'

Granddaddy tried to make Eamonn's mother sit up so she could drink some of the milk, but she kept on turning her head away as if it tasted bitter. 'But why didn't you go to the workhouse, laddie?' he said. 'Or you could have come to me. I wouldn't have turned you away if I'd known.'

'They only give out cornmeal porridge at night at the workhouse, and it didn't seem to do the baby any good. I asked them for some milk, but they said that first they have to feed the poor people who live there and they haven't even got enough for them.'

'Aye,' said Granddaddy, and his voice was fierce. 'Those people in London might have thought of sending food instead of soldiers. Isn't your father around to get food for you?'

'He's out looking for food now, sir.' Eamonn touched the baby's head gently again.

'He went somewhere a long way off. Thirty miles away. They said there was grain being given out. Would that be in Portumna, sir? He didn't know how bad the baby was before he went.'

Eamonn bent over the baby and was quiet. Then he said, 'They stopped paying the men on the works near the canal when the harvest came in. They kept saying the money should come soon, but there was no one to pay it out. And then they said no one should need government work any more since the harvesting

73

started. That's why my Daddy had to go looking for food, because they didn't give him any money and we didn't have anything to harvest, sir.'

9

The Roadworks

By the time Kate went to the post office to collect the letters a couple of weeks later, the Government had started the works again and there were some new clerks from England who were in charge of paying out the wages. All the scientists and all the officials they had sent to see what was wrong with the potatoes hadn't been able to solve the mystery and overnight the whole potato harvest had been blighted, the same as the year before. The Government set up new roadworks as well as the works by the canal, so all the hungry people who came into town from the countryside around could earn some money.

'Where they all sleep is a miracle to me,' Aunt Julia said, when she came to visit and stood in the kitchen watching over Kate's attempts to beat up eggs for a cake.

Kate already knew where a lot of the people slept, but she didn't like to say anything about it. She was afraid that if she told Aunt Julia or Granddaddy about the families she had seen lying in the ditches, with only a thin, ragged blanket to cover them from the rain, she would not be allowed to go into town alone any more. Aunt Julia was convinced that all the poor, hungry, people wandering the roads were just waiting to rob and murder her in the middle of the night, and she kept trying to persuade Kate's stepmother to keep the children at home all the time.

The gang of men on the new works just outside the town, on the Rickardstown road, were heavily guarded by a group of soldiers as if they were prisoners. As Kate drew closer she realized that it wasn't only men who were bending their backs and breaking up stones with old, worn-out hammers. There were women there as well, weary-looking creatures with thin, sunken cheeks. Their babies lay by the side of the road with scarcely a blanket to cover them.

A tiny black-haired creature, no more than two years old but already with the pinched face of a tired old man, toddled up to Kate and held out his hand, a habitual gesture, as if begging was a trade he had been born into. Kate gave him one of the coins her stepmother had given her and the little, barefooted boy, wearing only a ragged shirt, ran back to a woman working by the road and buried his head in her skirts.

Kate saw Eamonn working right at the end of the line. He looked stronger now, since Granddad had insisted on giving him and his family food every week. But he was as proud as his father. He had told his father and mother that he wanted to work because he didn't want to depend on Granddad's charity for any longer than necessary. And besides, he still dreamed of one day snatching his family away from the hunger that hovered around like a vulture waiting to devour them as soon as yet another potato crop failed. After he had to watch his little sister being taken ill and dying he was more determined than ever. Ireland was no place for the living – not unless you had a lot of money and a big warm house, like Kate's Granddad.

The weather was starting to turn cold again and Eamonn sometimes regretted selling the sweater Kate's stepmother had given him to keep warm. He knew that the gombeen man in Tullamore wouldn't give it back again unless he paid twice the money the man had lent him in exchange for it. But he had needed the money so badly.

He'd already had a letter from the place where one of his aunts used to live, telling him she had moved. When he wrote to the second address she had moved away from there too. He was convinced his aunt would help them if only he could get a letter to her. Now that he had her new address he didn't have any more money, and it looked as if it would take a miracle to raise the money without giving away his secret to his mother and father. Sometimes, when he felt like giving up the whole idea of moving to America, he closed his eyes and forced himself to imagine the joy on his parents' faces when he told them that they could escape at last.

Two weeks later, when Kate went past the works again on her way into Tullamore, Eamonn's whole family were out there working on the same site. His father and mother didn't look at her because they were spreading the boiling hot tar on to the road with rakes. Dermot was helping Eamonn to break stones with some of the other young boys.

'Everything costs even more now,' Eamonn's mother said, when Kate stopped to talk to them. She seemed to want to apologize to Kate for having the children out at work, when she had dreamed of sending them to school. 'Every week they put the prices up. And there's not that much to buy. People who've got the money'll pay even more than the asking price.'

She looked so ill and so very thin. Kate wondered why they let her work, those English men with nothing to do but sit in their warm little sheds and pay out the wages every day. Couldn't they see that she was so sick she should be at home in bed?

One of the men from the pay shed came over to them and told Eamonn's mother to get on if she wanted her money. He had a smart grey tweed suit and shiny black brogue shoes, so he didn't venture out onto the dirty road very often.

'I don't like to see Eamonn and Dermot having to do this,' Eamonn's mother said, picking up the next heavy bucket of tar. 'But they get fourpence a day, and we can't do without it.'

Shaun gave Kate a shy smile as she set off again on her way into Tullamore. He wasn't working, but he wasn't playing either. None of the children who were sitting there wanted to play with him, and the overseers would have shouted at them if they had run around too much. They just sat by the side of the road all day and waited for their parents to finish work.

'We had some blackberries yesterday,' Shaun whispered. You could almost see the taste of the blackberries smiling out of his face as Kate knelt down on the ground beside him. 'Don't tell anyone because there's still some more. Our Eamonn found them and he's the only one who knows where they are.'

Kate recognized the old flannel shirt that Shaun was wearing; it was the one Peter used to wear the year before. She supposed she ought to feel guilty, because her stepmother had done so much for Eamonn's family when Kate hadn't even asked her to. She had given them food and clothes and looked after Eamonn's mother when she was very ill, and all the time Kate had never given up trying to prove to her stepmother how much she disliked her.

Shaun was shivering in spite of the flannel shirt. It was the end of October and already unusually cold for that time of the year. 1846 was going to be the coldest winter Ireland had ever known.

Every week, when Kate went into Tullamore to shop for her stepmother or to collect their letters, the streets of the town seemed to get more and more crowded. The pavements and the narrow roads were full of people walking up and down, people who had nowhere to go until the time came for food to be distributed from the poorhouse. Some of them were poorer than others. The poorest of all were taken into the workhouse, but that was only if they could prove that they had no money, no land and nowhere to go. Granddaddy had even heard of people who gave away their land because anyone who had a plot of land, even if it was barren or covered with rotten potatoes, wasn't allowed to receive anything to eat from the poorhouse.

Eamonn's family were lucky to be taken on at the roadworks. People who couldn't get work had to carry the fear of starvation around with them everywhere they went. They stood in line for hours outside the poorhouse waiting for the time, once a day, when they were allowed in to eat a thin bowl of soup with a few pieces of cabbage in it. Kate had become used to the sight of children who were so thin they looked like old men and old men who looked like skeletons.

Her stepmother always made sure she had money to give to the poor people she met, as well as the money for shopping. So she had something for most of the tiny children with grubby faces who reluctantly left their places behind their mothers' skirts and ran over to her with outstretched hands and pleading eyes. But every week there were more hungry children. Why didn't someone do something? Kate didn't know what they could do, but someone should do something to stop the people starving.

While the poor people were streaming into the town, richer people were turning their backs on it. Every week Kate could see how many more people who had the money to escape had gone away. 'Rats deserting a sinking ship,' Granddaddy said.

Tullamore had once had a fine linen shop and a tobacco shop, as grand as anything in Dublin, people said. But the people with money to buy things had all gone. The good shops had gone too, along with the baker and the grocer. Aunt Julia said what a blessing it was that Granddaddy still had five sacks of flour so they could make their own bread. Even Kate could see that if they used their five sacks to feed the poor people who came begging up the drive to their big house it would be gone within a day and they would all have to starve as well. There were just too many people. Someone had to do something.

After walking back through town and having to shake her head and show her empty purse to so many poor people, Kate always walked home in a trance, scarcely noticing the autumn leaves that she used to crunch her way through, or the beginnings of a beautiful sunset, with a red like maple leaves brushing the sky.

One day in late October she was so deep in thought that she was already almost on top of the roadworks when she noticed that there was trouble again. She didn't pay much attention at first, when she heard the sound of jingling harness and the stamping of horses' hooves, but then she went round the bend and saw the soldiers, a whole crowd of them, high up on their horses, frightening the poor, tired people.

'For the love of God!' she heard a woman crying. 'There's a man dying here. Can you not help him instead of prancing around giving orders?'

There was a crowd round the man, who had collapsed from exhaustion and no one was doing any more work.

'He hasn't been paid for two weeks!' another woman shouted. 'He told me this afternoon. He came all the way from Galway because the pay clerks won't work there any more and the men didn't get any pay. He's walked all the way from Galway to work here. All he wanted was something to eat. He's not a troublemaker.'

Kate stood in the gathering gloom, clutching her basket. The horses pranced about restlessly, their hot breath making clouds of smoke in the cold air. With such a crowd of people around him, Kate couldn't see the man lying on the ground, but she felt compelled to wait and see what would happen. It crossed her mind that things might be dangerous, like that time when the soldiers shot people near the canal, but Kate wasn't afraid. She couldn't just walk away when there was a man lying there helplessly on the cold, stony road.

Ages passed and no one moved. The sky had turned blood-red. After what seemed like another age, the Captain nodded to one of the soldiers and the soldier got off his horse. He went over to where the man was lying and the crowd backed away to let the soldier get closer to the man on the ground. The soldier took his gloves off, knelt down and tried to open the man's eyes. 'The old woman's right,' he said. 'He looks in a bad way to me.'

Kate held her breath to try to stop herself crying. Did he mean that the man was dead? She wanted to close her eyes and shut out the deep purple blue of the sky. It made her cry when she looked at it. There was something deceitful and threatening about a sunset that looked so beautiful. What right had the sky to celebrate and put on its royal robes while some terrible unseen monster was creeping over Ireland, slowly strangling every living thing?

10

The Woman in the Snow

Kate's hands shook as she tried to open the letter from Boston without tearing the envelope too much. The postmistress in Tullamore would be sure to gossip about someone getting a registered letter from America. Kate looked all round before she took out the contents of the large envelope to see if anyone was watching her, waiting on the empty road to pounce on the girl with the registered letter.

She had never seen so much money. Everyone said her grandfather was rich, but she never actually saw his money and she had no idea where he kept it. The only money she ever saw was the money her stepmother gave her for the shopping and the small change they gave her to hand out to the poor people she met on the road. But in the envelope there was a twenty-pound note and an extra pound. How, on top of keeping the letters secret, was Kate supposed to guard all that money until it was time for her to buy her passage to America? The letter said she shouldn't sail until May, when the rivers were cleared of ice and the ships could get right through to Boston.

'I'm sorry I can't be with you on the voyage, my Katie,' her father said in the letter, 'but the money I've sent you should be enough for a first class ticket even if the prices go up in spring, as they're sure to do. You're almost a grown-up young lady now and you must look for a refined lady on the ship who'll look after you.'

The letter didn't say anything about when Kate would be coming back to Ireland. Perhaps he thought he had to get her away because of all she'd told him about the people dying of hunger. Kate couldn't believe that he would want Mammy and Peter and Joe to die of hunger, but he never said anything about them. She knew he didn't like Mammy any longer, but he wouldn't want her to die, would he?

Kate wished there was someone she could talk to, someone who would tell her what she should do. But she wasn't allowed to talk. He didn't want anyone except Kate to know where he was. So she kept his secret, and tortured herself because she didn't know what she would do when it came to May and he expected her to sail to America.

When the letters had first begun to arrive, Kate was proud that she was the one who had been singled out; she always knew she was his favourite. And at that time, when he told her he had gone away because he didn't like Mammy any more, she'd been pleased. She could have told him all along that he didn't need to get married again – and especially not to a lady who had been a schoolmistress and thought children were there to be ordered about.

In her first letter to him, Kate had really enjoyed shouting at him for leaving them and forcing them to live with an old, grumpy Granddad who only complained about how much it cost to feed the three extra children he had suddenly been given to look after. Then she'd demanded to know why he had left her to suffer under her stepmother if he couldn't stand her any more. But by the time she got the money, Kate wasn't so sure that she disliked Granddaddy any more and Mammy had been so kind to Eamonn and his family.

Every morning, when the others had gone down to breakfast, Kate counted the money. She had hidden it at the back of the bookcase in the children's room. Since she was sure no one else ever looked in her handkerchief drawer she kept all the letters there, so she could read them whenever she was left alone in her room. Sometimes, if Granddaddy didn't ask her to help with the milking, she managed to find time to read one of the letters after breakfast and put it in the pocket of her pinafore. Then, when it was time to put on her coat and go off to school she had the letters to keep her company all along the long, cold road.

From the beginning of November onwards it never stopped snowing. Kate had never seen snow before. All the old people talked of nothing but the weather. Stamping their feet indignantly, they said it never snowed in Ireland, when it was quite obvious that it could snow if it wanted to. The children weren't used to the cold and complained even when they had their coats on, so Mammy and Aunt Julia got out their knitting needles and tried to remember how to make woolly gloves. Kate didn't like the cold, even though she loved the way the snow made soft white pillows out of the green hills.

One of Kate's jobs was to herd the sheep every day from their pasture near the farm to a field very close to the school. Aunt Julia, who had lived in town all her life and thought Granddaddy was a country bumpkin, because he lived outside Tullamore, insisted that the paupers would steal the whole flock and that Grand-daddy ought to shut them up in the barn along with the cows and pigs, but he just shrugged his shoulders. 'You can't keep sheep inside,' he said. 'And anyway, we wouldn't have the room for them.'

'Have you ever tried getting a sheep to go with you when it hasn't a mind to?' Mammy said, shaking her head and then bending down again over her knitting. 'Those poor unfortunates wouldn't have the strength to run off with one of our sheep.'

So that was settled. None of the sheep were ever stolen. There were twenty at the beginning of the winter and twenty in February when Granddad and one of the men were out all night for the lambing. Kate did her job well.

It wasn't really strength you needed to get twenty sheep to move out of one field, down the lane and then into another; it was cunning. They were such stupid animals that Kate just had to find a way of convincing them that what they really wanted was to get up and move along the lane fast enough to reach the next field so she wouldn't be late for school. Kate dreaded the times when a convoy of soldiers came riding down the road towards her and the whole flock scattered in every direction, running down into the ditches or back up the road the way they had come. That always made her late. But when Kate was late for school she couldn't always blame it on the stupid sheep or the soldiers on horseback clogging up the road.

When it was especially cold and snowy, Kate loved to make each sheep get up from where it had been resting all night with a brisk, 'Whisht! Come on you lazy old basket!' just like she heard her grandfather saying to the cows. Then, as soon as the sheep had staggered to its feet and trotted shakily over the field to cuddle up to another sheep for protection, Kate would fling herself down onto the ground and roll around in the lovely warm spot left there by the sheep's body. Over and over, twenty times she would roll herself on to the warm grass and then jump up again to shout at the next poor sheep. No one ever saw her rolling in the snow and she never told Peter in case it made him want to share in the work. Looking after the sheep was her job.

As usual, Kate had left home at half-past seven. The school bell was due to ring at eight, but it was hard to believe the sun would ever rise on the new day. Kate's face was so stiff with cold that she was convinced she wouldn't be able to open her mouth if anyone passed her the time of day.

'Good morning,' she said to herself, by way of experiment. It didn't sound right. She tried, 'How are you?' But that was even worse. Her frozen cheeks refused to help her lips form a single round, warm sound.

She clapped her hands together to warm them up before she tried to open the gate to the field. The sheep were white splodges of cotton wool in the grey gloom. Kate cursed the gate and had to take her gloves off after all. The old rusty loop that usually flipped off the top of the gate post and let the gate swing open was frozen stiff and refused to budge.

Kate stamped her feet and blew like a horse, to warm herself up. The awkward old gate opened at last and Kate ran into the field, angry at the stupid sheep who were going to dawdle all the way to school and make her late. The cold of the deeper snow in the field gnawed at her toes, chewing holes in her two pairs of thick socks. She didn't know what time it was. There was no telling the time when the sky was as dark as the end of the world and every fresh fall of snow meant that the whole of Ireland could be plunged in darkness whatever the time of day.

Kate stamped her feet in the direction of the first sheep and managed to shout, 'Whisht! Move!' At least there'd be a warm spot where the sheep had been. At least she could warm herself up for a few seconds.

There were ten sheep cleared out of the field, most of them heading in the right direction down the road towards school and Kate was feeling good. Chasing around after the dozy, stupid sheep always warmed her up, though she never remembered how warm she would soon be when she first had to leave home in the morning. Her toes weren't cold any more and her face was warmed up enough to speak properly as she ran over to the group of five sheep huddled together at the far side of the field.

'Whisht! Come on you old women!' she said. They did look like funny old women, all lying so close to each other; their ugly black faces showed their disgust at the cheek of the girl for giving them such a rude awakening.

After Kate had done a lot more waving and shouting,

one of the sheep finally moved and the others started to follow her. As they did so, Kate thought she saw a wet, ragged old blanket on the ground just beside the dry place where the animals had been lying. Then she stood rooted to the spot, wanting to run away. It was a woman lying there out in the cold field; a dirty, ragged woman with hair matted like the wool on a black sheep's back.

Kate stepped back in horror but the woman didn't make any move to attack her. For a second, shorter than the time it took to register what she was thinking, Kate thought that the woman must be a banshee. In the same instant she shook herself and reminded herself that big, grown-up girls didn't believe in banshees. There was no awful wailing coming from the woman. No long, ugly fingernails stretched towards her to scratch her eyes out like the white ghost woman was supposed to do if she caught you. The woman lay quiet and still and when Kate plucked up courage to draw closer she saw that there was a peaceful smile on her lips.

Kate stretched out her hand. The woman was awful dirty, but Kate thought she ought to touch her at least. That was what she had seen grown-ups do when they thought someone was dead, to see if they were cold. She laid her hand gently on the woman's forehead. It was warm, hotter even than Kate's own hand. She drew her hand back as if she had scalded herself. If the woman wasn't dead, Kate would have to do something. She ran forwards to the gate and then back to the woman again. There was no question that she was alive. She opened her eyes halfway and smiled at Kate before she closed them again.

A hundred thoughts raced through Kate's mind when she didn't even know she had time to think. Why had the woman slept out there in the field? Was she mad? Didn't she know she could have frozen to death? There were the stupid sheep, half of them wandering down the road. Kate was halfway between home and Tullamore. Where should she take the woman to? If she ran off to get help it might be too late. The sheep had to come back into the field. She couldn't take the woman anywhere as long as they were running around.

The sheep all protested loudly at having to file back in through the gate again, when they had been looking forward to a helter-skelter gallop down the lane to the school field. When Kate had got them all to the far end of the field so they wouldn't go wandering out into the lane again while she was struggling with the gate, she put her arms round the woman and tried to heave her up into a standing position. She almost fell over backwards when the woman turned out to be lighter than Joe. Kate felt as if she could have carried her like a small child.

'Whisht!' she said very gently, as the woman flopped over to one side. 'Come on, deary. You can't stay here.' She remembered how that was the way her grandfather had talked to the sheep when they got themselves stuck in a grid somewhere and couldn't struggle free. He talked gently to make sure they didn't panic because that only made them get their feet caught faster.

'Come on, my deary.' Kate slowly made her way to the gate, half dragging, half carrying the woman.

There was no point in going home, Kate decided. Anyone could see that the woman needed a doctor and if she went home they would only have to send for the doctor from Tullamore. She might as well take the woman straight to the workhouse where they had their own doctor.

When they had got past the field the woman started to speak. Kate had to bend down to catch what she was saying, but it was all in Irish and they only spoke English at home. The only Irish Kate knew had come from talking to the men at the whiskey distillery when her father used to work there, but theirs was a different sort of Irish. The woman must come from a long way off.

'It's all right. I'll look after you,' Kate said, coaxing her to move on a little further. She couldn't understand why the woman was so very hot. Beads of perspiration glistened on her pale forehead. It was hard work for her to walk, as if they were climbing a steep hill instead of walking along a level country lane.

The matron at the workhouse was businesslike. 'You can leave her over there. She'll have to wait her turn.'

Her arm cut like a scythe in the direction of at least twenty other wretched bundles of rags crouching in the corner farthest away from her desk. 'They all say they're destitute,' she said, 'and how am I supposed to tell whether they are or not when they hardly speak a word of English? People ought to be made to learn English if they want to come to the workhouse. I don't suppose you speak their language do you, my dear? I could use a bit of help to sort this lot out.'

Her right arm sliced through the air again, just missing the heads of the people sitting huddled in the corner. She sighed. Things would have been a lot easier if she had been able to dispose of all the paupers at the stroke of a pen like the officials in England could. Instead of that, she had to try to talk to them and find out where they came from and whether they were really as poor as they said.

'I can't just leave her,' Kate said. 'She needs help now. I think she's really ill. She was lying in the fields out there.'

The matron looked suspicious. 'This isn't a fever hospital,' she said. 'The nearest place for fevers is Dublin. You'll have to take her to Dublin if she's got fever.'

Kate had never been good at lying, but she was learning.

'Oh, it's not fever that's the matter with her,' she said. 'She's just tired out. All she needs is somewhere to sleep. Then she'll be all right. Could *you* sleep out in a field with a pile of bleating sheep?'

The matron looked the woman up and down. 'They're tough these Irish, I'll say that for them. You're probably right. One night in here and she'll be on her feet again in the morning. Then she can get work and look after herself again.'

She didn't want Kate to think she was hard. 'They keep me that short of money, you see, my dear. I can't let everyone in, as much as I'd like to. But one night is all right. I'll tell you what, she can even have a bed today. Some of my women are out on the works. She can sleep all day in a real bed if she wants. I can't say more than that, now can I?'

Kate had brought typhoid fever to Tullamore workhouse.

11

The Curfew

Kate's brothers had been watching the driveway for a week and Joe had almost fallen out of the upstairs window twice, leaning right out to see whether there was anyone coming to the house. This year it wasn't only Granddaddy and Peter who were going to be fitted out with new clothes. Even little Joe was to have a new suit for Christmas as soon as the tailor came along.

The tailor finally arrived at the end of November and sat on the kitchen table in their house, stitching away and eating more than anyone could have imagined from merely looking at the man whose legs and arms resembled nothing so much as pipe-cleaners.

Next to eating, the tailor liked talking. 'I have a good life,' he used to say, with his mouth full of pins, as long as he didn't have to concentrate too much on threading his needle or measuring up a finished leg against Joe and poking him to make him stand still.

The tailor certainly didn't have a very hard life. He never had to carry anything except his scissors, tape and thread, since his customers provided everything else that he needed to make a suit. And on top of his wages of ninepence per suit he received a bed and as much food as he needed for as long as it took to do his tailoring. At least once in every visit, he would tell the family he was working for how he made a point of never going back to families who didn't give him enough to eat.

But of late, the tailor had taken to talking about others peoples' lives instead of his own. 'The things I've seen!' he said over and over again while he sat cross-legged on their kitchen table. He kept on saying it, like a needle stuck on a cracked old gramophone record, until someone finally pressed him to tell them a bit more about the things he had seen.

'I've walked the length and breadth of Ireland,' he said. 'There's not many can say they've walked as far as I have. Every year, for the last twenty years, I've gone the whole way from the Giant's Causeway to Skibbereen. But for the last two years it's been the same everywhere I've walked. There's no rich counties and poor counties any more. The whole country's in a bad way. Look at Tullamore! Look at King's County and Queen's County!'

He shook his head. 'The shops there used to be in this town!' Then he shoved a handful of pins into his mouth and took a long time fitting the sleeve into Joe's jacket, easing the material deftly so it would all fit in and not leave any wrinkles. 'The things I've seen!' he said again, shaking his head.

After that he refused to say any more. He said it wasn't a fit subject for children, starvation and death, and he wasn't going to talk about death as long as they were in the kitchen. If the tailor never did get to talk about the dead he had seen, it was because as long as they thought he had something to tell, none of the children dared to leave the kitchen. It wasn't that often they had a visitor who could say he had walked the length and breadth of Ireland.

One of the tailor's favourite games was to try and guess which families the different children were related to when they rushed into the farm kitchen and asked to play with Peter or Kate or Joe. 'Don't tell me, don't tell me, don't tell me . . . ' he would say, holding his breath and trying to guess as soon as a child put its head round the kitchen door.

He was proud of the fact that he had made suits for all the good families in Tullamore for the last twenty years. 'I remember your father couldn't stand still to be measured either,' he would say through his pinned-up teeth, when he had finally worked out which family a boy came from. 'You look the image of your beautiful mother,' he used to say to any of the girls who came in.

There was one exception to this rule. When Eamonn first put in an appearance the tailor didn't even try to guess which family he came from. He could tell at once that Eamonn's father had never ordered a suit from him. None of the families he had ever worked for had children who were so wasted away, so pale and thin.

It was the tailor's last day. He was embroidering the last of the thirty buttonholes he had made in three brand new jackets and enjoying the warmth of the kitchen stove and the hot tea that Mammy had just made for him. Suddenly an icy wind blasted through the back door and Eamonn rushed in, leaving the door half open.

'They've stopped the works again!' The boy flopped down on a chair, completely out of breath. 'Can't Granddaddy do something?' he gasped. 'More people will starve if they shut the works now. And none of us know who did it. They say that we all know and that's why they're closing it down. But nobody on our works did it, honest to God we didn't.'

Kate's stepmother scolded him. 'Why, child,' she said, 'you're half frozen. Did you not remember to wear that jersey I gave you? You shouldn't be out with only a shirt in weather like this.'

Eamonn shrugged and looked uncomfortable. 'There's none of the others has anything warm, Mrs. I feel bad if I'm the only one with a jersey.'

Kate had seen the jersey in the gombeen man's window and wondered why Eamonn had pawned it to get more money. She had forgotten to ask him about it.

'What's this someone's done that none of you know about? We ought to get to the bottom of this,' said the tailor. He could be as sharp as his scissors if he thought someone was telling lies, and he generally distrusted paupers.

'There's a land agent been killed just over by Philipstown,' said Eamonn. 'They found him lying dead on his doorstep this morning. Someone shot him and they say one of the people from the works did it. But we couldn't have, sir,' he pleaded. 'We were all out at work before sunrise. There's none of us could get their hands on a gun. And anyway, it wasn't us he turned out.'

'We heard about that.' Kate's stepmother pursed her lips as she handed Eamonn a big mug of warm milk. 'Drink that, child. They turned out fifty families over near Philipstown yesterday. God help us. The landlord's in England, so his agent did it. And now the poor man's been shot for his day's work. That's all the wages he'll get out of it. The landlord was probably down his neck for more rent.' She shook her head and sighed. 'And they say England's a Christian country.'

Eamonn's face was dirty and streaked with tears. He sat down at the kitchen table at the opposite end from the tailor and began to cry again. Kate went to put her arm round him. She felt useless and wanted to run upstairs and get her twenty-one pounds out from behind the bookcase. If only she could help him. If only her money would help.

'They say they're going to close the works until they find out who did it. But all the people'll be dead by then, Mrs. And there's hundreds and hundreds of soldiers. Philipstown's miles away. None of us could have done it, but they just won't believe us.'

'We'll see what Granddad can do,' Kate's stepmother said. 'Now you run along back to your Mammy and Daddy and take them something to eat. And I'll give you another jersey. I can't have you wandering around in the cold dressed like that.' She clucked like a mother hen. 'Child, child, child,' she said, shaking her head.

Granddaddy hardly slept that week. He persuaded

94

the priest and the Church of Ireland vicar and everyone else who was working to help the poor people, to go and see the officer in charge of the soldiers and the man in charge of the works, but they were adamant. They said that if they gave in, the people would have a licence to kill anyone who refused to give them food when they were hungry. They said no one would be safe to walk around Ireland without fear of getting shot. Even when Granddaddy told them that the murderer couldn't possibly be from Tullamore, they wouldn't listen. They said all of the Irish were dangerous – men, women, and children.

Granddaddy had never had any problems with the English living in his country. But there was one day when he understood why people got so angry that they could take up a gun and take someone's life. He had gone once again to see the officer in charge of the troops in Tullamore and stood before him, pleading with him to let the men get back to work. 'I give you my word of honour,' Granddaddy said. 'None of the men on the works had anything to do with the murder in Philipstown.'

The red-haired, red-faced officer leaned back in his red leather armchair and drew on his cigarette. 'You know,' he said, 'if there's one thing I've learned in this job, it's never to trust the word of an Irishman.'

Granddaddy went all the way to Dublin to speak to the man in charge of the Board of Works, but that didn't help either. In spite of all his efforts, it was only after many men had died, trying to walk to Dublin in search of food, that the works were reopened and the Government started paying out money again.

After the agent was shot the soldiers didn't leave the town for months. There was a curfew placed on Tullamore and no one was allowed out between sunset and sunrise. There was even a watch placed on Kate's house because Granddad had tried to argue with the Board of Works and they said he was a troublemaker.

He was working on the committee that tried to get more food for the people too, and the English said the relief committees were a way of covering up secret rebellions.

One night Kate was awakened by loud shouting. 'There's a curfew in Tullamore. Halt! I shall be forced to shoot if you don't stop. Who goes there?'

By the time Kate had shot out of bed and opened her window the soldiers billeted in the barn had all tumbled out to join the watchman. One of them was carrying a lantern, which he held up high to light up the face of the culprit. It was Mammy. Kate grabbed the eiderdown from her bed, wrapped it around herself and settled down by the window to watch what was going on.

'And where do you think you're going at this time of the morning?' said the sergeant in charge. He had been drinking whiskey and beer till the early hours of the morning and was not very amused about having his sleep disturbed so soon. His forehead felt as though it was being squashed down to his shoulders by the kind of wooden press they used to mash the hops for beer, and his brain went spinning round uncontrollably every time he had to bend down to Kate's stepmother.

The sergeant was at least six feet four and Mammy was a tiny woman, almost as small as Kate. Only her hat with its plume made of a turkey's feather made her look a little bit taller. Kate remembered seeing her laying the hat out the night before and polishing the soles of her shoes as well as the tops. The light of the lantern bounded off the bright, white blouse Kate had seen her starching and ironing before she went to bed.

'What do you mean by going out at this hour, mam?' the sergeant said. 'You know you're not supposed to. It's pitch dark, and my orders say there's a curfew from sunset to sunrise. That means nobody's supposed to go out. You're not going to make me shout at you, are you, mam?'

Kate smiled. She could tell that for some reason the great big sergeant was scared of Mammy. She reckoned it was because of Mammy being a teacher for so long before she got married. She never had to shout at anyone; she knew how to make people scared of her without even raising her voice.

'Young man,' said Mammy, 'I'm quite sure our good Queen Victoria did not give permission for a curfew so you could stand in the way of ordinary, law-abiding people like me going to say Good Morning to the Lord. They tell me Queen Victoria goes to church every day, so she won't want to stop me going. Holy Communion has been at six in the morning, curfew or no curfew, ever since I can remember. And if you don't mind I shall continue to go to church for as long as my legs are strong enough to carry me.'

Then she swept off down the lane, with her turkey feather waving proudly on her hat. The only thing the sergeant could do was to send her an escort. So two tall English soldiers, rifles at the ready, fell in behind her and marched off to the church.

Kate was proud of her stepmother. Forgetting the cold, she knelt down next to the open window, her elbows resting in the snow on the stone sills, long after the turkey feather had been lost in the darkness. Who else could have stood up to the soldiers like that? Kate wasn't even sure her father would have been so brave. He would probably have joked with them and then invited them all in for a drink; that was his way of doing things. He would have been too afraid to argue with them. Mammy hadn't needed to argue; she had just told them what she intended to do and then gone off and done it. Kate dared anyone to try to shoot her!

Kate thought of Eamonn and his family and of what would have happened to them if her stepmother and Granddaddy hadn't given them food and clothes and money. When she had written to America, asking for more money to help her friends, her father's reply was always the same. He didn't want her to go giving her money away to the paupers; they were the Government's responsibility. She must save up everything she had in case the ship's passage became even more expensive over the winter. He always said he was sorry, but it wasn't possible to get together enough money to help all the poor people in Ireland. If the Government in London couldn't do it, how could anyone else help them?

The only advice he was able to give Kate was that she should get away from the blighted land as fast as she could. The only money she received from America was the amount she needed for her passage out there. And instead of getting easier it was becoming harder and harder for her to decide whether to go or not.

She wished there was someone she could talk to about her father, but he had begged her to keep his letters a secret. She wondered how Mammy would feel if she did go to America. It wouldn't be right if she just disappeared, like her father had done. She would have to leave a note, explaining things. But what could she say?

A year ago, it would have been easy to write that she was going because she didn't belong in the family, because her father had married again without even asking her permission. A year ago, she could have written that she only wanted to be with Daddy in America. But now she had got to know them, Granddaddy and Mammy and the rest. And little Joe was her real brother, even though he had a different mother. She wondered how Daddy could have gone away and left Joe and Peter. Kate was sure she couldn't leave them. Why hadn't Daddy sent money for them to go to America as well?

Kate didn't notice the time passing. The sun had risen and still she stared out of the window, seeing nothing of the barn across the yard, her elbows resting on the freezing window ledge. 'Child, child! Will you go in at once and close that window? Are you looking to catch your death of cold?'

Kate laughed out loud and jumped up. She leaned her head right out of the window and shouted, 'I saw you, running off to mass with the soldiers this morning, Mammy.' It was the first time she had forgotten to use the word 'stepmother'.

The ridiculous turkey feather shook when Mammy laughed with her. She looked quickly round at the barn, where the soldiers were billeted, but nothing stirred.

'Child, will you watch what you say. We mustn't make fun of Queen Victoria's soldiers.' She tried to look serious. 'And the soldiers don't want to be looking at a young lady in her night-gown either. Now will you go in, and we'll have no more of your cheek!'

12

Knitting

Kate never listened very carefully when the vicar read to them, from the newspaper or his favourite poetry book. It was hard enough trying to concentrate on her knitting so that she didn't drop stitches and end up with huge holes in her work when she was supposed to be making something solid and close-knit to keep out the cold. If Kate had had any choice in the matter, she would have done her knitting at home in their warm kitchen, not sitting in Mrs Hennessy's grand parlour with half a dozen of the grander ladies from the neighbourhood who belonged to the Ladies Work Association. But she didn't have any choice.

It didn't seem fair. Although it was all right for the boys to spend their time hanging round the farm helping Granddad, Kate's stepmother wanted Kate to become a lady, and being a lady meant going to tea at least once a week with the other ladies of Tullamore.

Kate fidgeted and dropped one of her needles. Mammy raised her left eyebrow as Kate crawled around the floor looking under chairs and twitching at skirts to see if the needle had rolled underneath them. Kate glared back at her, forgetting how proud she had been of her stepmother only the day before.

It wasn't fair that she was the only one who was forced to sit there the whole afternoon. You weren't allowed to do anything at one of these stupid tea parties. You weren't even supposed to scratch your nose.

If only the vicar would choose something interesting to read like a real adventure story! But he didn't; it was always either a boring book of poems or the latest edition of *The Times* from London.

'Everyone knows the sullen apathy of dependence and can compare it to the sheer delight of personal achievement. Dependence on benefits from others corrupts the human spirit. We must stop giving out food to the Irish poor and encourage them to work for their living.'

The vicar slowly folded up *The Times* and smoothed it flat as if he had been given the job of ironing it before he thought of something to say. He knew they expected him to have some sort of commentary prepared whenever he read out a newspaper article. The moment he finished reading, every lady in the room looked up from her work. But they didn't want sermons. Mrs Hennessy had already reminded him that he was there to entertain the ladies while they got on with their needlework, making clothes for the poor.

'I suppose one must admit that there's a grain of truth in what he says. I suppose people might become lazy if you fed them all the time.' He frowned. 'Still, I don't suppose he'd have written this if he'd seen what things are really like here in Ireland.' Reverend Wood sighed and patted the few strands of reddish hair with which he tried to cover the bald circle at the top of his head. 'It's easy to say things like that when you're in London.'

The vicar propped himself up against the side of Mrs Hennessy's great marble fireplace. He was a small, worried looking man with a pale face and carrot-coloured sideburns. 'I might have said the same thing myself in a sermon, if I hadn't lived here for the last three sad years. None of my acquaintances in London want to believe how bad the famine is.'

Mrs Hennessy didn't like it when the vicar got too serious. He was supposed to entertain the ladies by reading to them so they could get on with their work. She didn't want the Reverend Wood telling her she

101

should have a bad conscience. Mrs Hennessy was doing all she could for the poor people, providing tea once a week for the Lady's Work Association while the ladies all sat in her parlour and knitted warm clothes to give to them. And she helped out three times a week at the soup kitchen which Kate's Granddad had started, serving thin soup to the masses of people who flooded in from the countryside all around. Mrs Hennessy didn't see what else she could do.

'They might send more money for the soup kitchen, I'll give you that,' she nodded. 'We could make it a sight more nourishing if the Government sent us some help.' She went back to her knitting, an exquisite lacy pink cardigan for a baby.

Kate had found her needle and was knitting again. She hated knitting, but she wanted to do something to help people and Granddaddy wouldn't let her near the soup kitchen. He said he didn't want a child to see the people fighting over food. Kate groaned out loud; she had dropped two stitches a few rows back. She would have to try harder if she wanted to get even one garment finished.

Mammy had seen to it that Eamonn's family had enough warm clothes. But there were always other families, barefoot little girls begging in the cold and rain, or mothers with babies and no shawl to wrap them up in. Kate wished there was some way she could make shoes for the little barefoot children.

She didn't often join in the conversation when her stepmother took her along to the Lady's Work Association. The ladies were all so grand that she was sure she would say something stupid.

But Kate couldn't stop herself answering Mrs Hennessy. 'My Granddaddy says the Government wouldn't have needed to send us anything. He says we could have had enough barley to keep the soup kitchen going for six months if they hadn't sent all the grain to England after the harvest.'

Kate was shocked at her own courage. She blushed and bent her head down over her loose, shapeless piece of knitting.

Mrs Hennessy looked her up and down sharply, and glared at the holes in her knitting. Only a girl who knitted so badly would contradict a remark made by her elders and betters. Kate didn't look any older than twelve. How could she know about things like the price of barley? Mrs Hennessy's grain had been shipped off to England along with all the rest, under military protection. Her eyes were reduced to tiny lines as she scrutinized Kate from head to toe and wondered whether Kate actually knew about Hennessy's barley being sent away. The child had always made her feel uncomfortable, the way she stared at you when you were talking, with those grey, accusing eyes of hers.

Mrs Hennessy smiled. She didn't want to spoil her tea party by having words with Kate. 'Who would have paid the price for grain round here, my dear?' she smiled. 'It would have just rotted away in the granaries and no one would have bought it. You wouldn't want the landowners to be turned into paupers as well, would you? What would have happened to the poor people then?'

Kate had no answer to that question. All she knew was that someone should have done things differently. She felt the vicar must be right because he said the same things that Granddad always said; if the people in London would only come and see for themselves what things were like, they would be forced to send more help.

When Kate next saw Eamonn and his mother on her way to school, they told her that Eamonn's father wasn't working out on the road with them any longer. The group of men he was with had been moved to the workhouse to help in building a fever shed. The matron had given up trying to send fever cases to Dublin; almost every one of the workhouse inmates had fever.

First the men had to build a large wooden shed in a field a short distance away from the workhouse. When that wasn't enough they had to build another one. People were arriving every day from the countryside round about and there was only one doctor to look after them. The town doctor had moved to England and there was only the workhouse doctor for the whole of Tullamore, a young man who had been in the town for two years.

When the Government wouldn't give him any more money to build another fever shed, he had ridden round to all the big houses, begging. With the small amount of money he managed to raise there was no chance of building another fever shed. The workmen had to construct shelters for patients to lie on the bare ground by resting boards against the side walls of the workhouse. When even more patients arrived, the army gave the doctor some tents to put the fever victims in. And still the poor, sick people kept on coming.

The workhouse matron was one of the first to contract the fever. After she died, the two nurses who had been helping her packed up their bags and left. The people were very sick and needed a lot of care, so the doctor had to go begging again, to find some nurses. As soon as he came to Kate's stepmother and asked if she knew of any young girls who would be prepared to work as nurses in the fever sheds, Mammy decided to go herself.

Everybody warned her not to go. The ladies at Mrs Hennessy's shook their heads and warned her that she would be the next to die of fever but all she said was that the Lord would protect her. She annoyed her friends by refusing to listen to their warnings and she continued to annoy the sergeant by breaking the curfew every morning and going to church before she went on to the workhouse. Kate thought she was wonderful.

The fever was everywhere. People said they were finding it more and more difficult to breathe. They thought the fever was hanging like a poisonous gas in the air all around them. No one was safe. The two Catholic priests who went in and out of the workhouse to visit the sick both contracted the fever and died within two weeks of each other. Mrs Hennessy died, and she had never been any closer to the workhouse than the soup kitchen which was at least five streets away from the fever sheds. People panicked. Was the whole of Ireland going to die before anyone in London did anything?

On some winter days when the air was so cold that it seemed to grow thick and stagnant, Kate imagined that she was breathing in the fever too. But she was most scared about Mammy, working so close to the sick people in the workhouse, and now she knew she couldn't get rid of her fears by buying herself a first-class passage to America and going to live with her father.

For the first time, people were leaving for America in the middle of the winter, when everyone knew that the ships couldn't possibly get through to their destination till spring because the estuaries were frozen. Nobody seemed to care. The only clear idea in their heads was that they had to get away from their doomed country.

One day Eamonn came to see Kate with the letter that had finally arrived from his aunt in Boston. He waited till Granddad had gone upstairs before he took the thin piece of paper out of the crumpled envelope.

'See what she says?' Eamonn pretended to smile. He had got used to coping with hardship and tried to make a joke out of disappointments. He put his cap on the table and tucked into the bowl of porridge Granddad had ladled out for him. Kate could see that he wasn't in the mood for joking.

'I wanted to keep it all a secret,' he said, blowing away at the hot porridge, 'but there's no reason to any more. I'll never get that kind of money.' Kate read quickly.

Eamonn's aunt said there would be work for them if they managed to get over to Boston. They were always looking for able-bodied Irish men who could do a good day's work for a good day's pay, she said. She was sorry she couldn't help them with money, but she had lost her job a few times and hadn't managed to save anything. She said she was looking forward to seeing them all in spring when the bad frosts had gone.

'I kept writing letters,' said Eamonn, 'but they never got there. All my letters got sent back because she moved house so much. But I didn't want to give up. I had to sell my jerseys to the gombeen man when I needed the money for more stamps and paper.' He sighed. 'I used to dream about the look on my Mammy's face when I went to her with a great pile of money from Auntie and told her she didn't have to worry any more because we could all get away to America. We won't be going there now.'

When you make a house out of cards, you have to put each new card on the pile very, very carefully so that the rest of the cards don't all come tumbling down. The only way Eamonn could stop himself crying was by placing his words as carefully as cards, scared that his feelings would make his house of cards collapse. He didn't want Kate to notice how badly he felt. He reckoned he'd done enough crying in front of her.

Kate reached out and put her hand over his. 'Something might turn up,' she said. Perhaps she could tell him her secret about the letters from Daddy. Perhaps Eamonn could tell her what she should do.

Then the door opened. Mammy was home from the workhouse. As soon as she saw Eamonn she began to pack a bag for his family, with Kate helping her to get the things out of the larder.

Kate was just coming in from the dairy with a hunk of cheese when she stopped and said, 'Yes, that's it!' Suddenly she saw very clearly what she must do.

'What's it?' asked Mammy. 'What are you talking about now?'

Kate shook her head and smiled. 'I wasn't thinking.'

She couldn't tell Eamonn about it as long as Mammy was around. Kate couldn't wait to see his face when she told him that she had the answer to all his problems. She didn't have to ask Eamonn for advice about her journey to America any more. There was no longer any doubt in her mind.

Kate was ready to rush off down the drive as soon as Eamonn's bag was packed. She opened the door and the cold air blew a merry breeze full of dancing leaves and snow into the kitchen. 'I'll just walk down to the end of the lane with Eamonn,' Kate said.

'Child, what can you be thinking of? You've only a thin dress on and I am not having you gallivanting around the countryside with a young man at this time of day.' Mammy wiped her hands, put on her white apron and started to scrub carrots in the bucket of water near the sink. There was never any arguing with her, but this time Kate tried, just in case.

'O, Mammy,' she cajoled, 'it's only to the end of the lane. I promise I'll come back when we get to the end of the lane. And anyway, Eamonn's not a young man. He's only twelve.'

Mammy threw more carrots into the water and sprang out of the way as they plopped in and sprayed water all over the floor. 'It's not Eamonn I'd be worrying about, child,' she said. 'It's just not safe to be out, with all those English soldiers hanging around the place.' She smiled at Eamonn. 'Now run along on, laddie. I want you to be getting home before the curfew catches you. You can come back again tomorrow, you know. No need to stand there gawping like a great big loon.'

Eamonn thanked her for the food and then closed the kitchen door carefully behind him.

Kate was angry with Mammy. She had been thinking about telling her the secret, but that would have to wait. Kate longed to tell her how she was going to help Eamonn, but perhaps she wouldn't be pleased. She wondered how Mammy would react if she suddenly blurted it out. 'Daddy isn't dead. He's in Boston and he wants me to go there and live with him. Only me and no one else.' That would be a good way to annoy her. Except that Mammy wouldn't show she was annoyed. She never did. It was never much use trying to annoy her.

'There's something I didn't want to tell Eamonn.' Mammy handed Kate a knife to chop the carrots. 'But that's why I wanted him to hurry on home. He'll find out soon enough, poor laddie.'

'What's the matter?' Kate pretended to be bored.

'His poor daddy came into the fever shed today with a fever he must have had for days. He tried to keep quiet about it so's not to worry them. There's not much hope for him, Katie.' She carried the heavy saucepan over to the range. 'God bless us! I don't know what's going to happen to those poor children. That poor woman. I wouldn't be surprised if they all catch it now.'

Kate wished she knew why she could never trust her own feelings. Only two minutes ago she had been burning with a stinging hatred for Mammy. She had already started to think again about how much better things would be if she went to America, where no one would be bossing her around, telling her what to do all the time. Only two minutes ago it had seemed that all Mammy was good for was giving her orders and calling her 'Child' when she was already twelve and almost grown-up. It was Mammy who forced her to wear too many skirts to keep her warm, and thick, scratchy woollen stockings that were always falling down as soon as Kate began to break into a run. It was Mammy who made Kate go and sit and knit at the Lady's Work Association, even though Kate would have much preferred knitting at home to being on her best behaviour and listening to the gossip of those silly old women.

Now Kate saw her stepmother differently again. She didn't know of anyone else's mother who would have gone to work in the fever shed, cleaning all the poor people who hadn't had a wash the whole time they had been wandering the roads. There were lots of people helping out at the soup kitchen, but you didn't have to touch the people when you were serving out soup. You could stand on the other side of a wide serving-hatch and shout at people when they pushed someone else to get at the food. Mammy had been good to Eamonn too, and anyone who was good to Eamonn was bound to be Kate's best friend.

She couldn't bear to think of Eamonn catching the fever, but things looked bad. There was no escaping from it. Nearly everyone died a few days after its black shadow fell on them; the poor people died quicker than the rich because they were already weak from hunger and cold. Most of all, the poor had had enough of fighting against misfortune and just didn't want to struggle any more. But rich people died of the fever too.

'They ought to keep away from him,' Mammy said. At last she sat down by the big deal table and took hold of Kate's hand. 'It would be best if all the relatives stayed away from the fever shed when they have someone in there dying. All they do is catch the illness themselves. The poor sick people don't recognize anyone who goes near them, God bless them.' She shook her head. 'But they will keep coming, flinging themselves on the ones they love and crying and kissing them. If only crying and love could save them.'

Mammy hardly ever talked about her work in the fever shed. She usually kept quiet about it because Granddaddy was so worried about her working there. But now she seemed terribly tired and sad.

'Perhaps they won't die, Mammy,' Kate said. 'You've done so much to help them. You've given them so much love.'

She shook her stepmother's hand, as if she was weaving a magic spell with every word. 'Perhaps they won't die.'

13

Fever

It didn't seem right that spring should come that year, when nothing had changed for the better. It didn't seem right for the sun to shine so brightly that Eamonn, in spite of himself, began to hop and skip along the road to Kate's farm. Then he stopped to watch the lambs in Kate's fields. If they had only known what sadness was hanging over the workhouse, they wouldn't have been leaping up into the air like that.

Eamonn didn't think of the lambs as something to eat. The only meat he had ever eaten was the bacon they used to cook with cabbage. It seemed like years and years since someone in Ballinglas had killed a pig and they had had a great feast. He chewed on dandelion leaves that had started to shoot up by the side of the roads and grumbled to himself again that the lambs had no right to be so happy. No one had the right to be happy.

Six times the doctor had thought his father was getting better and six times he had had a relapse. Every time Eamonn's father looked as if he was going to recover, they had all been so proud of him for fighting the illness, but now everyone could see there was no strength left in him. Eamonn considered the scolding he could have given his father if the poor man had been able to take notice of anything people said to him; after all, it was Daddy who never stopped telling them they must look on the bright side of things. He'd even told them not to give up hope on that terrible day when the agent had told them their house had to be tumbled.

'At least he came and told us a week ahead,' Daddy had said, when first Mammy and Grandma and then all the little ones had burst out crying. 'It could have been worse, asthore. They might have come and thrown us out in the middle of the night, without any warning.'

Eamonn had been bursting with pride and happiness the week after his father caught the fever because at first it looked as if his father was the only one who was going to beat the illness. The doctor and Kate's mother said they had never seen anything like it, the first time Daddy started to sit up in his bed. He was cheeky to them and kept on saying, 'I don't know what they're keeping me in here for. I'm as right as rain.'

'He must have a strong constitution, in spite of everything,' Kate's stepmother said when she reported the news of his recovery to her excited audience back at the farm.

But after the fourth relapse, the doctor began to shake his head and say that he'd heard of cases like that, and the end was always the same. It was just a different kind of fever. You thought people were going to get well and then they had one relapse after another. There really wasn't any hope.

Eamonn wanted to stand over his father and shake him back into the fight. He wanted to shout, 'Don't give up, you silly old fool! It could have been worse!' He realized he was shouting at the lambs. 'You could have had the other kind of fever and snuffed it right away. You're the one who always says we shouldn't give up.'

Eamonn was still angry at himself because of the baby dying. It just hadn't made sense. One day he had been able to coax a smile out of her, even though she was hungry like the rest of them; the next day there had been no more smiles. It was like that with his father. He had been sitting up in bed the day before, saying he'd be out of the workhouse before they knew it. Then, when Eamonn had gone to see him in the morning

Kate's mother had put her finger on her lips and told him he could only stay with his father for two minutes. And Daddy hadn't even recognized Eamonn when he tried to speak to him. He'd given up.

'He's a filthy, rotten coward,' Eamonn shouted at the lambs and then wiped his eyes on his sleeve. 'A rotten old fool of a coward.' But, since he wasn't interested in joining in their games, the lambs had begun to ignore him.

Kate didn't know what she could say to Eamonn if his father died. She knew how badly she had felt that time her father disappeared and she was left to fend for herself with a stepmother she had determined not to like. At that time she had no idea what had happened to her father, but she still felt angry with him. It was his fault that they were forced to move out of the manager's big house next to the distillery right in the middle of Tullamore. He was to blame that Kate suddenly found herself out in the country with a grandfather she had only met once, at her father's wedding. And there had been no one to talk to about how angry she was. People had kept on telling her that even if her Daddy was dead she was lucky to have a Granddaddy who was kind-hearted enough to take in his widowed daughter with her three orphan children.

Kate sometimes wondered if she would still have been angry with her father if she had had to watch him first get sick and then slowly die, knowing that she couldn't do anything to help. She never allowed herself to think about what she would feel if Mammy caught the fever. It was a black thought that sent her head spinning till she was dizzy.

During the last two months Kate had kept on worrying that Eamonn could catch the fever as well. She tried to persuade him not to visit the workhouse so often, but there was no keeping him away. Every day he walked out to the farm to tell them that his father was getting better or getting worse. He couldn't think of anything else. The only way they could help was to feed him and give him food for the rest of the family, because Mammy said that if they could get enough to eat and regain their strength there was less chance of them catching the fever.

Granddaddy had started slaughtering the cows, one by one, to provide meat for the soup kitchen, but extra food was no good to Eamonn's father. The fever made him thirsty, but he couldn't eat. No one could understand how a man who had been so close to starvation could survive. The doctor shook his head every time he went to see him and saw Eamonn's mother sitting patiently by his bed. 'That woman has it harder than anyone else,' he used to say. 'She keeps on hoping he'll get better. It's cruel to give them any hope.'

It was Kate's job to stay at home and mind the other children in the house whenever there was no school, because Granddaddy was out at the soup kitchen. They were all sitting round the kitchen table doing their schoolwork when Eamonn knocked at the door. As soon as he came in Kate began to warm up the porridge that had been left on the stove.

Joe and Peter were glad to have an excuse to interrupt their work. They grinned at Eamonn. He always had some new joke to tell them when he came round. He collected jokes in his head wherever he went, to entertain the little ones. Then Joe and Peter would repeat them over and over again, usually getting them wrong, until Kate got sick of stupid jokes and told them to hold their tongues.

'Tell us a joke, Eamonn,' Joe pleaded. He was a round six year old, with a face made even rounder by the fact that Granddad used to put a pudding bowl on his head and cut round it once a month, giving him a haircut like a red-haired cherub. His jerseys, handed down from Peter, were always far too big for him and Mammy made him wear a couple of vests underneath them so he looked even more well-padded.

Peter could tell that Eamonn was in no mood for jokes. 'Ah, will you leave him be, Joe,' he said. 'He has to get his breath back first.'

Eamonn had run all the way up the drive, wanting to rush into the kitchen and cry, 'Our Daddy's going to die.' But as soon as he opened the door he felt that it wouldn't be right to trouble the younger ones with his problems. He sat there in silence, watching the steam rise from his bowl of porridge.

Kate didn't need to ask about Eamonn's father. She knew instinctively that something was wrong, so she sat there without saying anything either. She pushed her schoolwork away to the other side of the table and watched Eamonn, waiting for him to speak.

Joe and Peter were too scared to say anything. They knew how angry Kate could get when she looked serious like that. There was no talking to her. They both put their heads down and concentrated on their homework. The writing they did after Eamonn came in was better than it had been in a long time.

The old grandfather clock ticked wearily away like a very old man dragging his feet. Time shuffled along and still Eamonn sat there and didn't want to go home. He didn't want to hear the bad news. He thought perhaps he wouldn't go home at all. Then he would never need to hear that his father had died.

They heard someone running through the yard. Peter flung down his slate. 'Finished,' he said, 'and I don't care what she says about it. I'm not doing it again.'

Kate took one look at the smudges on the top of Peter's slate and knew that as soon as Mammy came in he would be doing the work again, but she didn't feel like having an argument with him. It was easier to tell Joe what to do.

'You'll have to be writing that again, Joe.' She didn't want him to get so annoyed that he threw his slate against the wall and broke it as he had done once before, so she spoke quietly to him. 'Can you just write these little fellows over again, Joe? Mammy'd like them better if you did them a tiny bit neater.'

Then the kitchen door opened and Dermot walked in with a big grin on his dirty, sweaty face. He looked as if he had run without stopping the whole way from Tullamore.

'Daddy's all right again, Eamonn,' he panted, 'and he's been asking where you are. You'd have punched him on the nose if you could've heard what he was saying about you. He sat up in bed and said, "Where's that gallivanting son of mine? Is he off charming soup out of the parish ladies again?" He remembers everything, Eamonn. And there isn't a trace of the fever on him. You have to come and see him now. He's asking for you.'

Dermot stood with his hand on the door knob and the kitchen door half open, ready to run all the way back just as fast as he had come.

But Eamonn was weary. He didn't believe his father was going to get better any more. These times when he seemed to get better were just cruel. The doctor had said so. There was no hope. Eamonn found himself wishing that his father had been taken while he was away, after all. It was just too painful to drag himself back into hoping for the seventh time. Even the doctor had said he couldn't survive.

'You've got to go and help him fight, Eamonn,' Kate could see his reluctance to move from their warm kitchen where he had been trying to forget everything for half an hour. The bowl of porridge was still untouched. 'Come on, you great coward. It's harder for him. If he can fight the fever, so can you.'

Eamonn hit hard with his hand against the high rough wall which sheltered the back of the workhouse from the road. He hit hard with the heel of his hand and felt no hurt. He felt nothing.

'I'm not going to cry.'

He heard a strained, small voice and knew that it was his own, although his teeth were clenched tight shut. His hands writhed and twisted into fists and the fists hammered against the rough wall, plastered with glass and sharp stone, so that it slashed and cut his knuckles. But he did not feel that his hands belonged to him. He felt nothing.

'I'm not going to cry. I'm not going to cry.'

Dermot and Eamonn had run back into Tullamore as fast as they could, with Dermot already so tired that he had to keep slowing down to a walk. They arrived a minute too late.

Kate's mother looked up quickly as if she was about to scold them when they ran down the central corridor of the long, quiet room, gasping for breath and ready to collapse near Daddy's bed. The quietness felt warm and peaceful like the quiet of their hut in Ballinglas after Grandma'd been trying to get the baby to go to sleep for hours and she'd just closed her eyes. Eamonn saw Mammy sitting on the floor beside the low, narrow bed, holding Daddy's hand. But she didn't look at him. Then he saw Kate's mother lift the edge of Daddy's blanket and he saw his father's eyes, open.

As he stared at the bed, the noise of running feet broke the quiet, drumming in his ears. But it was a noise that no one else heard. Only Eamonn heard the sound of his own feet, running and running along the long road, down the cobbled alleyways and along the cool, stone corridors of the workhouse. He watched Kate's mother gently closing Daddy's eyes with one hand while her other hand slowly pulled up the blanket to cover his face. And far away, he heard the sound of the pickaxes and huge hammers crashing into the roof of their hut. He heard the men shouting and fighting and the children wailing as the English soldiers chased them along the road away from Ballinglas. While Kate's mother was straightening the blanket all around the bed, moving gently and quietly in the quiet room where all the fever cases came to die, Eamonn's ears were tortured by the cries of all the dead people on the road out of Ballinglas.

Eamonn was hungry for silence. He wanted to go where there was no crying, no sharp, cutting voices and screaming children, but once again the sound of running feet invaded his thoughts. Kate's mother quietly finished smoothing down the blanket and came towards him, her sadness making her eyes glitter in the shadowy room. The drumming sound of running feet on country roads, on cobbles, on cool, stone corridors hammered on inside Eamonn's head, faster and faster. He should have run faster. He turned and ran out of the room.

The others were still in there, with Kate's mother. But Eamonn wasn't going to let her see him cry. She wanted him to. They all wanted you to, the people in the workhouse, the people outside. They wanted to see what you looked like when your Daddy had just died. They wanted to see you cry, to see if you were different from all the others who watched their fathers die. So they hung around like vultures. And when you caught some old women watching you, they said stupid things, pretending they were there to comfort you. 'It's for the best, you know. And he's with the angels now.'

'I'm not going to cry.'

Eamonn's voice was louder. He threw back his head and opened his mouth wide, gasping for air. But his eyes were closed, squeezed tight shut to shut out the brightness of the blue spring heaven. He wasn't going to let them see him cry, those old women who lurked at the workhouse gates, longing to pray for the dead. They must have been willing his Daddy to die, those black-clad vultures. They'd been waiting for the chance to stare at him and say, 'God bless you, laddy', when they saw him run from the room.

People would say he shouldn't have run away but he had to run. The room where Daddy was alive and then dead, all in a minute, had closed in on him, ready to suffocate him. And he'd had to get away from Kate's mother, with the sorrow in her eyes. What right did she have to be sad, to share his sorrow. He wasn't going to let her see him cry so she could feel sorry for him. Not her. And not the old, pious vultures with their rosary beads. Eamonn shuddered. He knew why they stood fondling the shining black beads at the gate to the workhouse, not to say prayers with them, but to count off the dead. Every bead on their rosary was a hundred dead men.

'I'm not going to cry.'

There was a fierce man inside him, a big, angry giant, not Eamonn, who roared like a bull in pain. With every word he screamed, he hammered his fists against the rough wall and the stones scratched and hammered back at him. But his body felt nothing. He hammered again to wipe out the memory of the old women in black who had been standing at the gates of the workhouse when he ran out. He had wanted to kick them and fling them out of his way.

Someone should have saved his Daddy. The doctor or the priest. A man like Daddy, a man who had fought back against the fever so many times, he didn't deserve to die. There was no reason why he should have died. Eamonn was angry at Kate's mother. He thought of the way she had looked at him with her sorrowful eyes, pulling up the sheet with her left hand, while her right hand made sure that Daddy's eyes were closed for ever.

'I'm not going to cry.'

Suddenly, pain gripped both of Eamonn's hands and started to crush them. A giant of pain, an English giant, like the sergeant who'd tumbled their house, was pinning Eamonn's hands down – crushing them beneath a landslide of heavy boulders. The English had guns, the big, brutish bullies. There was nothing he could do against the English.

He gave up his hammering, and his broken hands dropped down by his side. He stepped back, away from the wall and looked up at the broken green glass on the top of it as if he were seeing glass for the very first time. Slowly, his clenched fists relaxed. Like a clumsy puppeteer, Eamonn raised his hands to look at them, one by one, as if they were on strings and didn't belong to him.

He was staring at them still, not knowing where the blood and bruises came from or why his hands should ache so much, when his mother came round the corner with Dermot.

'Mammy!' he said. He held up his hands to show her, as he always used to show her his cuts and bruises when he was a little boy in Ballinglas.

And he didn't try any more to stop himself crying.

14

A Time to Cry

There wasn't much time for crying. Eamonn had to find a job. And not just a boy's job, carrying the boiling hot tar for the men to spread along the road. That only earned you enough for one bowl of porridge. Eamonn needed far more money than that. He frowned as he strode out along the south road away from Tullamore. No one else was going to die if he could help it.

'There's been enough people dead,' he shouted at the road, that was strewn with boulders and wound away ahead of him like a knotted string of grey woollen blankets.

'My Granddaddy'll give you food. Don't worry,' Kate said, when Eamonn went to see her after his father had died. But Eamonn wanted to do just what his father would have done, and Daddy had never wanted them to be beggars. All he had wanted was work, to feed the family and pay for a roof over their heads.

Eamonn quickened his step. And as he walked, faster and faster, he was sure he heard his father walking behind him, saying, 'There's no law against hard work. Everyone should have the right to work. A good day's work for a fair day's pay.'

Eamonn longed to stop and turn round and talk to his father, but something kept him walking, faster and faster. He wanted to ask his father if he remembered the time they had all day-dreamed of the jobs they would get in Dublin. Before Grandma died in Tullamore. But when he did manage to turn round his father had gone.

'Enough!' Eamonn shouted. 'Enough!'

No one heard him, not even a skinny old sheep or a cow. The road was deserted.

All the big houses Eamonn had been to were deserted as well. And there was no one left to tell him where the people had gone to.

Six times, Eamonn had left the road and walked up the long driveways, past the empty barns and the dirty, broken windows of abandoned farmhouses until he got to the big house where he thought he might find work. And six times he had seen straight away, as he rounded the bend nearest the house, that the place was empty. At the upstairs windows, shutters, like the gagged mouths of kidnap victims, gave away no secrets. Only the broken windows on the ground floor told their spiteful tales of desperate children stealing jars of plums from the housekeeper's larder.

At the sixth house, an indignant door, yanked out of all but one of its hinges, creaked and groaned at anyone who would listen to its story of two children who had slept there for a month, till the larder stores were all gone.

In a downstairs window of the seventh house, a flicker of yellow candlelight danced with the rays of the setting sun.

An old woman answered the door.

'Would you be the messenger from England?' She looked like an excited child. 'I don't often have visitors from England now, you know. Such times we're having.'

'No, I'm an Irish boy.' Eamonn felt bad when he saw how disappointed she was, and he didn't know what to say next. Now that he was standing close to the front door he could see that the big house was in a far worse state than the others he had called at. He could tell at once that there wouldn't be a job for him there, but he needed something to say.

'I was wondering.' He felt so stupid, he twisted his fingers nervously behind his back. 'I heard there might be some work up this way,' he lied. 'I need to find a job so I can feed my family. A good job.'

The old woman nodded and smiled, encouraging him to go on talking, and Eamonn suddenly wanted to tell her everything about his life. Even though he had never met her before, he knew she would understand the hard times they had had. 'I need to find a really good job, so I can get enough money to take them to America.'

He paused, out of breath, as if he'd just recited a long poem without stopping. There was something scary about the place. He thought he saw something moving at the window above the front door, but there was no one there.

When he looked at the old woman again, she was still smiling. 'Aren't you a grand young man, thinking of your family like that.' Her smile was gentle and welcoming. 'Wouldn't any mother be proud of a son like you?'

Eamonn smiled back. 'Our Mammy can't do so much work,' he said. 'She was ill, and so I've got to look after her.'

The old woman nodded sympathetically and smiled. She seemed to know about Daddy. Eamonn could tell that she wasn't going to ask him about Daddy and he was grateful. He didn't know why, but he felt that if she, of all people, asked him what had happened he would break down and start crying all over again. There was something different about her. She wasn't a vulture, not like the old biddies outside the workhouse.

Something about her reminded him of Kate's mother, but she was older, much older. Her hair was as white and shiny and delicate as the white china teacups they had in Kate's house. Eamonn remembered the time Kate had shown him how the china teacups were so fine that you could see through them if you held them up to the light. There was something of that about the old woman standing in the doorway, something fine and beautiful and fragile. She was wearing a green dress with a white lace collar.

He was still thinking of Kate holding up the white china teacup to let him see the light glowing through its pearly side when the old woman said, 'Will you not come inside for a cup of tea?' Eamonn almost laughed, and nodded. 'I've no work for you here, and you've a long journey back. Isn't it the West of Ireland you come from?'

'Not so far,' said Eamonn. The front door creaked shut behind them and he followed the old woman along a dark corridor. 'We've lived in Tullamore this last year.' Their feet made a squeaking noise on the highly polished floor.

At the end of the corridor, the old woman flung open a double door and they were out in the light again, the warm light of the sun just as it was ready to set outside the enormous windows.

'This is the lounge, where we used to have visitors.' She showed him to one of the sofas near the window. 'We had a lot of visitors here, when I was younger. Parties where people came from miles around. Everyone wanted to come to our parties. We kept an excellent cook in those days.'

A frown threatened to take over her face but she shook it off and said, 'Now all the people have gone.'

'I'm so glad you've come to see me.' Her sudden smile was like a rainbow after a thunderstorm. 'I've always liked visitors.'

She stood with her hand on the door handle. 'I don't use this room any longer. Not now we don't have so many visitors. But I said I'd make some tea! You must be parched!'

She hurried away, and Eamonn heard the squeak-squeak of her footsteps as she went towards the kitchen at the front of the house. The kitchen must be the room right next to the front door, where he had seen the candle. As soon as the old woman had gone, Eamonn stood up and looked out of the huge windows which stretched from floor to ceiling.

'I thought Kate's Granddaddy was rich!' he whispered. Either because the light was fading, or because the gardens were bigger than anything he had ever seen before, he could not see where the sweep of lawns and statues and flower beds ended. Graceful flights of steps led his eyes into the distance, where tall trees made patterns of black lace against the sky. What the fading light also hid from view was the weeds, slowly choking the wonderful rose beds, and the green and brown drops of water that trickled from twisted, rusted bits of piping where fountains had leapt and danced in the sunshine when the old woman was young.

'Would you believe it?' The old woman was standing in the doorway again and Eamonn shot back into the chair she had first given him. 'I haven't a tea-leaf in the house.'

'It doesn't matter really. I can drink water.'

'It should be coming along any day now. It's my son who sends me the tea from England. This house belongs to him, you know.'

'It's a beautiful house,' said Eamonn. 'I've never seen a garden like that.'

The old woman shook her head. 'Ach! I don't have the gardeners I used to. My son says we don't need to keep up a grand garden so long as he's living in England.'

She stood with her back to Eamonn, looking out of the window. 'My garden's not what it used to be.'

Once again, Eamonn found himself thinking that if she stood with her back to the light he would be able to see through her. Then she whirled round and clapped her thin white hand to her forehead.

'My goodness! What will you think of me, neglecting my visitors like this?' She giggled. 'You can tell I don't have many visitors any more, can't you? I'll go and see if I can find you some cake. I'm sure I have some cake. I always keep my special fruit cake in, just in case some-one comes.'

Eamonn got up again when he heard her scurrying towards the kitchen. He wanted to look at the books crowded on shelves all around the walls. There were curving steps for climbing up to the top shelves, but Eamonn stayed down on the floor, tiptoeing slowly over the deep, soft carpet and stroking the beautiful leather bindings of the massive old Bible and encyclopedias. He smiled as he thought of what Daddy would have said. His father always wanted him to have a job where he could read lots of books.

'I'll swear I had some cake only yesterday!' The old woman had opened the door quietly and stood there with her hands on her hips.

Eamonn told her he wasn't hungry, but she was still exasperated. 'It's a very special kind of cake!' she grumbled. 'I sent my son all my fresh eggs, and he promised he would get his housekeeper to make me some more cakes. They should have been here a long time ago.' She sighed. 'Would you believe it? He's taken my last housekeeper to England with him. Says I don't need one because I don't have so many visitors.'

She went towards the window again. 'It's getting darker,' she said. 'You'll have to be going soon. I'll just find you a couple of plain biscuits to fill you up till you get home.'

Eamonn felt suddenly weary and noticed how hungry he was. He sat back in the huge, green leather armchair next to the fireplace. 'I thought Kate was rich,' he whispered, and his head started to spin as he craned his neck to look up at the crystal chandelier hanging from the high ceiling.

This was the kind of house where Grandma had dreamed of them all finding work. Eamonn remembered Daddy and Grandma laughing and joking as they tramped along by the canal.

'They've all so much money, they don't know what to do with it,' he heard Grandma saying. 'I can sew fine dresses for the ladies and you can look after their horses and carriages.' Eamonn clutched the arms of his chair. His father had said, 'Aye, we could all live well if we work in one of those big houses.' The house was alive with their ghosts.

He heard the kitchen door slam and the squeaking of feet along the corridor and then the old woman came into the room. She was holding a heavy stone jar with both hands. When she sat down near Eamonn and lifted the lid off the jar, he knew it would be empty.

'I'm beginning to wonder if there are mice in this house.' She smiled. 'I can't believe it. Not a plain biscuit in the house. I'm going to have to write to my son and tell him to send me some tea and cake by the next post.'

She leaned towards Eamonn and whispered, 'My mother used to say, "Never marry a miser!" Well, I didn't marry one. It's my son who makes sure I have no money to spend.' Eamonn nodded, but he didn't really understand what she was talking about.

'You wouldn't believe it,' she said, 'but he takes all the money out of this place. Doesn't leave me a penny. He expects me to go a-begging whenever I need something. And even then he will keep on asking me, "Are you sure you can't do without your tea, Mother? It costs me a pretty penny to keep you in tea."'

There was only a small speck of daylight left. The old woman sighed and put down the empty biscuit jar. 'I don't mind all that really. He's sold the farms and he's sold my carriage and now he's taken my housekeeper away. But the thing I'm really worried about is that he might sell the house as well. It's his house, you know, but it's the place where I was born. Last time he came, he told me I didn't need such a big house just for myself.'

She clutched Eamonn's arm. 'You don't think he'll throw me out on the roads, do you?'

Eamonn was horrified. 'No one would throw an old lady like you out on to the road, with nowhere to go to.' He thought of Grandma, stumbling along the road and sleeping in the cold fields on the way to Tullamore. But he didn't say anything.

'No. Perhaps you're right.' In the half-light, the old woman looked like Grandma. 'He won't make me leave my home at my age.' She stood up and moved towards the door again. 'You know, I feel awful, not giving you a bite to eat. I'll just go and have another look. I must have something in the house.'

But Eamonn saw how dark it was getting and thought of the lonely road back to the town. 'I'm all right. Thank you, I'm all right. I'd better be going now, before Mammy starts to worry.'

The old woman didn't want him to go. She picked one of the red, leather-covered books off a shelf near the door. 'Let me just show you a picture of my son. He's not such a bad laddy really. He's as handsome as his father was before him. Look.' Eamonn saw a tall man with black hair and a huge moustache which made him look like an opera singer.

'He has hundreds of men working for him,' she said, turning over the pages. Eamonn didn't count the men, but the next picture was of a very large group, standing in front of a big steam ship.

'He has them working on the docks in Liverpool and the Ship Canal in Manchester.' Eamonn recognized the old woman's son even before she pointed him out on the big photograph; he was the tallest man in the whole group.

'It's because of his work in England that he wants to sell this house,' she said, pushing one stray corner of the photograph back into place. 'There's always ships he wants to buy and new business he wants to do. They tell me he's going to earn a pile of money one day.'

Eamonn's eyes went wide with excitement, as the ghost of an idea stared out at him from the photograph. 'D'you think he would give me a job?'

15

Kate's Gift

Kate had twenty-one pounds stuffed inside her undershirt. At every step she took she heard the money rustling, scolding her for letting her father down. He had sent the money so that she could take a first class passage and go to live with him in his fine house in Boston. What would he say if he knew she was going to give it away?

She looked anxiously back at the man who passed by with his donkey, wondering whether he had heard the money rustling too, but he had been too busy shouting at the animal, trying to get it to keep moving. The water barrels on its back had been banging about like the booming drums in the soldiers' parades. He couldn't possibly have noticed.

As soon as the donkey had rounded the bend, taking its drumming water barrels and the shouting farmer with it, Kate felt that the accusations of the rustling new pound notes were getting louder.

Daddy had written that he had lots of money in America, much much more than they had ever had in Ireland. He had talked about the wonderful school he was going to send her to, where the nuns wouldn't let you past the front door unless you had a lot of money and your Daddy had a good position. Daddy thought it was a huge joke that the Mother Superior had actually asked him, 'And how many servants do you keep?' before he had been able to register Kate for the school. But Kate was registered and expected to start school in Boston in the summer. The pound notes scolded her for letting him down. On the other hand, if he had so much money he shouldn't really miss twenty-one pounds. Perhaps he would send her some more money when she wrote and told him what she had done. Somehow she had to make him understand how badly she needed to help her friends.

Something else kept on nagging at Kate, worrying her even more than the rustling, scratching pound notes in her undershirt. If Daddy really had as much money as he said, Kate still couldn't understand why he hadn't sent any more when she had written and told him about all the starving people in Ireland. In answer to all her letters he had just kept on writing that he had done all he could by giving money to the collections they had in America for the starving Irish. But he could have given more, couldn't he, someone who had enough money for the best school in Boston?

Kate had walked along the lonely road from the farm to Tullamore hundreds of times before, but it had never occurred to her to be frightened. Now she was terrified that she would be robbed before she got to her destination. She hugged her arms tightly around her chest, trying to stop the rustling noise, but that didn't work. The road was empty, as far as the eye could see but the rustling of the pound notes made the air jump up and down like a wild wind blowing through the trees.

Kate stopped and looked all around, wondering whether there was someone waiting in ambush, lying down by the side of the road in the ditch.

The closer she got to Tullamore the more people she ran into. She passed a woman, sitting by the side of the road, holding out one hand. The other hand was supporting a baby who was trying to feed at her breast. A tiny child, no more than two years old, lay beside her in the dirt, sucking its grimy thumb.

Kate gave the woman a halfpenny and the rustling money scratched at her heart when the woman smiled and said, 'God bless you, asthore.' With twenty-one pounds, the woman might never have to sit out beside the dirty road again. But there were so many people begging by the roadside. Before she got to the post office Kate had given out all the halfpennies her stepmother had saved for her.

Miss Doyle, the postmistress, gave Kate a knowing, slightly disapproving look as she handed over the letter from Boston. A child of Kate's age shouldn't be getting so many letters from so far away. Miss Doyle had often wanted to ask whether Kate's stepmother knew about the letters. She had already decided to mention them when she next saw her at church. Miss Doyle had begun to form her own opinions about who the letters might be from and if her suspicions turned out to be true she was sure Kate's stepmother wouldn't be too pleased.

It was impossible to get any information out of Kate. She had finally learned to keep secrets.

'What's the betting you're the next one who takes off for America?' the postmistress said.

Kate felt as if Miss Doyle's raven sharp eyes were picking away at the bodice of her dress, uncovering the money and her guilty secret. She blushed and shook her head. Then she put her grandfather's letters into the pocket of her skirt and went outside, still clutching the letter from Boston.

The rustling of the money in her undershirt was definitely getting louder. She should have thought of a better place to hide it. There were so many poor people waiting around outside the post office, with hands outstretched. Was it right to use all that money for one ship's voyage instead of feeding the people?

One night she had heard Granddaddy talking to Mammy about the soup kitchen. He had collected fifty pounds for one week, and still that wasn't enough. Who did have enough money to feed the poor people? Granddad said the Government in London were the only ones who had enough money and they didn't want to part with it.

She read Daddy's letter as she walked along the pavement. After every sentence she had to stop and shake her head sadly when children came up and asked her for money. It was such a cheerful letter. That was what the old ladies of Tullamore had liked so much about Daddy. He had always been the one to keep them laughing until their sides ached. He used to get very annoyed if anyone got too gloomy about anything.

'Don't be going round with a face like a graveyard,' he used to say. In his letter he told Kate she wasn't to worry about her friends any more. 'You've done a grand job helping them through the winter,' he wrote, 'but now that it's spring they can begin to plant their potatoes again and by the summer they'll all have so much to eat they'll be bursting out of their skins. The good Lord won't let the potatoes get blighted another year. You don't have to worry your head about that.'

Kate was annoyed with him. Sometimes she wondered if Daddy even read half the things she wrote to him. It was hard enough doing the writing too, on the window ledge in her room by whatever light came in from the moon. She'd told him time and time again that Eamonn's family had been evicted from their land and they didn't have a patch of garden to grow their own potatoes on. She'd told him how many other poor families there were with no land and no work.

When she read the next part of his letter she was even more exasperated with him. He wrote, 'Who knows? If your stepmother wants to carry on giving them something to eat now and again after you're safe and sound here with me, perhaps we can send her some money and then she can tell them it's a present from you.'

'Daddy, you must be soft in the head,' Kate said under her breath. 'How can you send money over here to Mammy and Granddaddy when you don't even want them to know where you are?' She had reached Eamonn's house and quickly read to the end of the letter before she pushed open the front door.

'Have you ever eaten ice-cream, my Katie?' Kate didn't even know what ice-cream was. 'Well, there's a grand place here in Boston that I'm going to take you to as soon as you arrive, where there's nothing but fine ladies and gold chandeliers and ice-cream as far as the eye can see. It's like a fairy-tale palace, my Katie, and I'll be taking my princess there the very day she comes to Boston.'

In the long, dark hallway Kate took the crumpled notes out from underneath her clothes. Then she counted them before she put them back into their envelope. Twenty-one pounds. This time she knocked at Eamonn's door before she pushed it open. She was glad to see that he wasn't there. His mother was sitting up on the mattress that Granddad had brought round with his horse and cart, and letting Shaun slide up and down her bent knees.

'Hallo, Katie!' she called. 'Have you heard the latest from my Eamonn? He only wants to take us all off to England and get himself a job on the Manchester Ship Canal.' Kate noticed that there were lines of grey in her black hair; Aunt Julia always said a death in the family made people go grey.

Eamonn's mother shook her head and made Shaun stand on his own two feet on the floor. 'Just like his father! He'll never stop dreaming.'

'But they do say there is work in Manchester and Liverpool.' Kate rushed to defend Eamonn.

'Won't you sit down now?' Eamonn's mother said. 'There may be work on the moon for all I know, but it's getting there that's the problem. Have you any idea how much it would cost to take me and the children to Manchester? And we'd have nowhere to go once we got there. Why, we know more people in America than we do in England!'

She pointed to the end of the mattress and patted it to make Kate sit down. 'Well, are you staying, or aren't you? It's a long walk back to the farm and you all alone,' she said. 'You should rest yourself while you can.'

She picked up one of the little jerseys that Mammy had given her and started darning a hole in it.

Kate sat down at the end of the mattress, but she was embarrassed. She didn't know how to tell them about her gift without them falling all over her, thanking her for her generosity.

Eamonn's mother didn't give her a chance to talk. 'I mean, if we landed in Boston, there'd be two of my sisters waiting to meet us and all ready to find jobs for us and all. At least there I'd know someone would find a place for us to sleep. But we don't know a soul in Manchester, unless you count this man Eamonn's heard of who's something big in the Ship Canal. And he doesn't know us. So who says he'll give Eamonn a job anyway?'

She laughed, 'Amn't I the silly madam, boring you half to death with that kind of dreaming talk? I told you Eamonn was a dreamer, just like his father. You might as well talk of going to the moon, really.'

'I've just brought this for you,' Kate said and held out the registered envelope she had been keeping since the money had first arrived. 'You mustn't ask me where I got it, but I didn't steal it; someone gave it to me.'

Dermot and Shaun crowded round to look over their mother's shoulder but Kate still held on to the envelope and didn't show them what she'd brought.

'It's enough for all of you to go to Boston if you buy a cheap passage. I asked the man at the canal locks. Granddaddy says he knows everything about trains and things. And he says nobody should need more than this. He says there's a boat from Dublin every week. But please, you mustn't tell my Mammy or my Granddaddy where it came from. The person who gave it to me doesn't want them to know.'

Shaun, who didn't appreciate riddles and was impatient to start the game of using his mother's knees as a slide again, held out his hands, 'Aw, come on Mammy! Play with me again, Mammy!'

Suddenly, Kate put the twenty-one pounds into Shaun's outstretched hands, turned and ran out of the door.

When she was already well away from the house and still running, she bumped into Eamonn, coming home from his day's work near the canal.

'Hey! Did your Granddad tell you he lent me one of his books?' He was really excited. 'I thought I'd forgotten how to read since we couldn't pay a schoolmaster any longer, but I read it all last night. I sat out on the front step as long as the light lasted. You better tell your Granddad I'll be coming round to get another one soon. He says I can borrow as many as I want. He's the best old man in the whole world. And you tell him that from me.'

Kate smiled. Her Granddaddy was an expert at hiding the good things he did. 'I've just been over at your house,' she said.

She felt shy and couldn't think of anything to say. 'I–I sometimes forget that your Mammy and Daddy could only speak Irish when you came. Your Mammy can speak the English as well as most people now.'

Eamonn laughed. 'Daddy was the best. Our Mammy says he could have learned any language in the whole wide world. She used to say if there was one thing he couldn't bear, it was keeping quiet when other folks were talking and telling stories.'

'You'll all need to speak English if you go to America,' said Kate. 'They say there isn't a soul there who speaks Irish.'

Eamonn shrugged his shoulders. 'Ach, we'll be all right here now,' he said, 'as long as I can work and get us some money to live. And Mammy'll be strong again soon. Perhaps she'll be strong enough to go to England. If I can get the money. They say there's work in Manchester, on the Ship Canal. They say it's hard work, but it'll do.'

He drew circles in the dust with his bare foot. 'Perhaps when I'm grown . . . I'll find money to go to America . . . they say it's a grand place . . . but we'll be all right here. Or in Manchester, I suppose.'

Kate's stomach did a cartwheel with happiness. Eamonn still wanted to go to America. He always tried to hide his feelings when he felt bad about something but she could tell he still wanted to go. She skipped all the way home, her imagination painting the scene that would be taking place in Eamonn's house and then painting it again, twenty times over.

'You're the cat that got the cream,' said Mammy, after she had watched Kate smiling to herself and forgetting to eat her porridge that night.

'I think the Kennedy's are going to go to America,' Kate said.

'Well, that's news to me.' Granddaddy wiped the porridge away from his white bristle of a moustache. 'Eamonn was in here only yesterday, asking me how he could raise the money to go to England to find work. And then when I said that would take him a good year or two, he was saying he was going to read his way through all the books in my shelves. He won't manage that if they're away off to America.'

'But how on earth are they going to get there?' asked Mammy.

'In a ship,' Joe said with his mouth full.

'No, I mean, where will they get the money from? I've heard you'd need at least eighteen pounds for a family of six and there's the four of them. Where in the world will they get so much money?'

'Oh, some aunt in America sent it,' said Kate. 'Eamonn kept on writing to her and telling her how bad things were and now she's saved up enough money. I

136

met Eamonn today and he told me.'

Kate had an idea how she could make her story even more plausible. 'I never told you before, Mammy, but Eamonn had to write so many letters he used to pawn the warm jerseys you gave him, at the gombeen man's, just so's he could buy stamps.'

Mammy nodded, 'So that's why he was always walking around in all weathers in his ragged shirt, God bless him. He's a grand young lad would do a thing like that for his family.'

16

The Tiny Green Frog

When Kate looked out of the back door she realized it must be late. The sun didn't start to set until eight o'clock at night in June and the sky was already the colour of dark blue delphiniums, with just a touch of pink and gold right down near the ground as if someone had arranged the delphiniums in an enormous vase with pale pink and red-gold roses.

Kate didn't have to worry about the curfew. There hadn't been one for a couple of months now, not since the warmer weather had made food a little bit easier to find and the landowners had stopped worrying that they were going to be murdered in their beds. Still, it wasn't often that Mammy was home after sunset.

She was usually home by the time the pigs had begun their squealing and the old mare had started to drum her hooves against the barn door, protesting that it was about time someone came and fed them. Kate didn't need to go back into the house and look at the clock in the hall to tell how late it was. The animals told the time well enough. Granddaddy could have set the clocks by the minute the pigs began to squeal, about an hour before their feed was due.

Granddaddy and the boys were in the barn. The pigs had stopped their noise as soon as they were fed, and some of them were already snoozing, resting their long, lazy, sausage-shaped bodies protectively on top of the troughs of half-eaten mash. They snored contentedly and their ears twitched to chase off the flies. Everything was peaceful. Granddaddy was letting Joe wield the huge fork to push some grass through the bars to the bull, so Peter was the first one to see the little frog.

'Hey, Granddaddy! Will you look at that fellow!' he shouted. 'Look at him go! Whoo!'

The tiny frog, the colour of new-mown grass and not the dry straw stuff they were feeding the cows, took one more leap to be well out of the way of Joe's monstrous fork and then cowered in a corner, not knowing what to do next.

'Let's take a look at him, Joe,' whispered Granddaddy. 'Lay the fork down over there. Careful now. Don't frighten him.' They all crouched down, getting as close to the frog as they dared.

'Will you look at his tiny black eyes!' breathed Kate. She had never seen such a small frog before. It was a real jewel, the colour of fresh, green leaves, not mottled and grey-brown like the nasty, stone-coloured old toads they saw down by the canal.

Joe's eyes grew rounder. 'Granddaddy,' he whispered, 'd'you think he's a prince?'

Peter whooped with laughter and in a flash the frog was gone, but he couldn't stop himself laughing. 'And Kate's the one who has to kiss him,' he giggled.

'Ah, will you look at that now,' said Granddaddy. 'You've scared the poor mannikin out of his wits.'

They didn't see the frog any more after that, so Granddaddy and the boys went on forking the grass to the cows. It was quiet enough to hear them chewing away, keeping time with Granddaddy as he did his milking. Kate went off down the driveway to look for Mammy.

She wondered what Eamonn was doing. He had told her he would write from Dublin as soon as they knew when their ship would sail to Boston, but Granddaddy said the ships' captains could never say exactly when the voyage to America would be. It depended on the weather. And it depended on the ship. Granddaddy didn't tell Kate what he had read in his newspaper, that some of the ships people set sail in were in such a bad state that they never even arrived.

Kate stood looking at the long line of yew trees; it was only four weeks since she had raced up the drive with Eamonn the day he had come to say goodbye. She remembered because it was the first time he had ever beaten her in the race. Mammy had been pleased to see him and his family looking so strong and well. She said they needed their strength for the long voyage.

Kate could hardly wait for a letter to come, but Granddaddy kept telling her that four weeks wasn't long. It could take as much as eight weeks to get one of the cheapest passages to America and even then perhaps Eamonn wouldn't have the time to send them a letter straight away. But Granddaddy had promised Kate he would take her to Dublin to see them off on their long journey. It was hard to be patient.

Once she had reached the white gateposts, Kate didn't have to wait long. Even though it was almost dark, she could tell Mammy from a long way off because she walked more quickly than other women.

Kate ran along the road to meet her. 'Hello, my Katie, I'm an old stop-out, amn't I?' Mammy took Kate's hand and they walked back to the farm together without talking.

Now there were no roses in the sky, only the deep blue delphiniums, but Kate could just catch the scent of roses and new-mown grass as they walked up the drive.

Mammy went into the barn and told Granddaddy why she was home so late.

'Young Dr Lawrence has gone down with the fever,' she said. Granddaddy left off milking a cow and came round to the front of the stall.

'You hold the bucket, Joe, there's a boy. Hey! And mind she doesn't kick it, there's a good laddie.'

'They won't find anyone else happy to work in a place like Tullamore workhouse when so many poor people just come there to die.'

'He's got it so bad?' Granddaddy asked.

Mammy shrugged her shoulders. 'He isn't strong, after all these months of waiting up every night. Maybe he'll try to fight it, like Eamonn's Daddy. I don't know.' She picked up her straw hat and went inside to the kitchen. Kate followed her.

Mammy hung up her hat, went upstairs to change her dress and then laid out her shoes ready to polish them for the next day, the same as she always did. Kate watched her, wondering why she didn't say anything more about the doctor's fever. Suddenly, fear clawed at her spine, and she put her arms round her shoulders as if she could fight off the cold fear by curling up into a ball like a hedgehog.

'You're not going to die, Mammy, from the fever in the workhouse?' She felt she had to whisper; Mammy had been so quiet and sad since she got home.

Her stepmother shook her head. 'I won't be dying for a while yet. There's too much to be done to think about dying.' Then she smiled, a small, shy, mischievous smile.

'But tell me, Katie. The truth, mind. You wouldn't have anything to worry about, now would you, if I wasn't here any more? You'd always have him to look after you.' Mammy motioned with her head over her shoulder, like people always did when they were referring to relatives in America, as if their relatives were in the next room instead of thousands of miles away. 'You'd always have him over there, wouldn't you now, Katie?'

Mammy turned round to get her long, white apron from the back of the door. Kate stared at her, speechless. So she knew that Daddy was alive. But how did she know? That old gossip, the postmistress. Had she read the letters and told Mammy what was in them?

'Ah now, Katie.' It was as if Mammy had already read her thoughts. 'You know I wouldn't go reading your letters. I don't know what he's been saying to you.

But I do know the hand of the man that I married. Why were you always leaving those letters in your pinafore pocket at washing? And didn't you wonder how they got there when I just used to take them out of your pocket and leave them on your dresser? I didn't want to say anything, you know, as long as you didn't want to talk to me about it.'

Kate blew out all the breath she'd been holding. How could she have been so careless? 'He wants me to go to Boston,' she said. 'He sent me a lot of money, twenty-one pounds, for a first-class ticket. He said he didn't want me to travel with all the poor starving people running away from the hunger and I was to get a nice lady to look after me on the journey.'

Kate's stepmother didn't say anything. She took off her small, silver-rimmed spectacles and blew on them. It sounded as if she had been holding her breath as well. She rubbed the spectacles on the corner of her apron. Kate had to say something to break the silence.

'He wants me to go to a fine school for girls in the countryside near Boston, and then I'm to live with him at the weekends. He has a fine, big house and a house-keeper,' Kate said. 'He says America's a very grand place and he never would have had so much money here as they pay him there.'

Her stepmother got up and fetched one of the oil lamps from the dresser. She polished the lamp slowly with the corner of her apron, before she carefully lifted off the glass chimney and lit the wick. The flame flared up, bright purple, before it calmed down to a pale yellow. Mammy's face glowed as she bent over the light, adjusting the wick so that it didn't get wasted and burned up too quickly. She looked up at Kate. Her face and the little wisps of hair that always struggled out of her tidy braids were golden in the lamplight.

'America would be a fine place for you to be, my Katie,' she said softly. 'They say there's nothing you can't do there if you set your mind to it.'

She sat down on the other side of the table behind the lamp. Kate had never noticed how beautiful she was before, the only woman for miles around with hair like ripened corn and eyes as blue as the flowers that bloomed in the cornfields.

'But I'm not going to America, Mammy!' Kate jumped up and flung her arms around her stepmother's neck, laying her head against the old blue cotton dress she put on every night when she got home from the workhouse. 'When Eamonn and all his family set off for Dublin, it was Daddy's money they had for their tickets. I gave it to them. I'm staying here with you.'

17

The Nimrod

Just as Eamonn thought the steep, slippery, winding wooden steps would go on for ever, his feet stumbled against a rough, wooden floor and the voice of the sailor who'd been showing them the way to their part of the ship called out from behind, 'Right, this is your steerage. Your bunks is the ones with the same numbers as your tickets.'

Eamonn wondered just how anyone expected them to read the numbers on bunks or tickets. It was so dark, deep down inside the ship. But it wasn't the warm, peaceful sort of darkness that Eamonn loved to feel around him when he stood in Kate's barn. It was the kind of darkness that smells of mould and sickness, of damp washing that will never dry and dirt so cleverly hidden away in deep, dark corners that no one will ever find it. It was the kind of darkness where people die, quietly, so as not to cause any trouble, and where bodies can be quietly spirited away and dropped over the side of the ship into the ocean. It was a darkness that smelled as if it held as many secrets as the ocean waves all the way to America.

The darkness deep down in the hold of the ship had its own sounds as well. Eamonn heard the weary, mithered voices of mothers telling their children, over and over again, to be quiet or the sailors would throw them off the boat. He heard dark, choking, rasping coughs and the snores of old people, already so exhausted by their long trek to the harbour that they didn't even dream of going on deck to take a last look at Ireland.

The ship's engines weren't moving, but the darkness vibrated with sound, with the noises of babies crying and small children moaning. Sometimes the voice of a ship's steward boomed out, 'Stop that Godforsaken row!' and the darkness would fall silent for a few seconds before the babies forgot the threatening voice and remembered once again that they were hungry.

Eamonn had never been on a ship before and none of them had known what to expect. When they heard that the cheapest tickets said STEERAGE on them, his mother and Dermot thought this meant they would be up near the captain watching him steer the ship. Daddy would have known what it really meant.

Eamonn's eyes got used to the darkness and he turned round to smile at his mother. He wasn't going to let her see what he thought of the place they would have to live in for the next six weeks.

'Would you look at all these people!' Mammy squeezed her way along the passage between the narrow bunks. Not a single berth was free. The bunks, with their straw mattresses, were stacked three tiers high and from every bunk bright eyes peered at them from pale, thin faces. Eamonn would never have believed he could get used to such darkness, but soon he could see quite far in the gloom and he realized there were two more rows of bunks behind the ones on either side of the central gangway.

As he looked at the people penned in on all sides by the wooden bunks, he remembered the one time in his life when his Daddy had taken him to a cattle market. He didn't remember how old he must have been then, or how they'd got there. All he remembered was sitting on Daddy's shoulders looking round at rows and rows of cows in pens, as far as the eye could see, all of them moving about restlessly, moaning and mooing and kicking with their hooves against the wooden pens, cooped up in a space that was far too small.

'But where did all the people come from, Mammy?'

whispered Dermot. 'There's more people here than in the whole of Tullamore.'

'They came from Dublin,' said Shaun. 'Just like we did.'

They passed the central space where the big cooking pots were set up ready to dish out a ration of broth once a day to all the passengers. They squeezed their way through more gangways crowded with the belongings of families sleeping two to a narrow berth. Mammy smiled and said hello to the people they passed, but children scuttled away behind their mothers' skirts and the mothers only nodded without smiling.

Right at the end of the narrow central gangway, in the darkest part of the hold, they found their own two bunks. 'Well, at least we've only got the noise from one side to worry about.' Mammy dropped the blanket full of food from Kate's stepmother onto the bottom bunk. 'It could have been much worse,' she said.

Eamonn thought he was going to suffocate. Kate's mother had told them how healthy the sea air was and how it would make them all look better than they had done for years. But the air that Eamonn could breathe was full of the smell of sickness and the sweat of a thousand bodies crammed into the dark, creaking hold.

'I'll just be off up on deck again, Mammy,' he said. 'I've a feeling Kate and her Granddaddy will be waiting on the quay until the ship sails.'

Mammy looked around. From where they were, they could see the next three or four rows of bunks in any direction, but not much further. 'I'd be afraid you'd get lost.' She had her hand on the blanket of food, clutching it tightly. 'I'd like to go with you now. To say goodbye. But I can't leave all this. What do you think, Eamonn?'

Eamonn was desperate to get out into the fresh air, out of the foul-smelling hole where he knew he would have to sleep. If he had had any choice at that moment, he would have left the crowded ship and begged Kate's

Granddaddy to take them all back to the farm with him. But there was no choice. Daddy had never wanted them to be beggars. If they stayed in Ireland, they would always have to beg Kate's Granddaddy for help. In America, they'd have jobs to go to and money and food of their own.

He forced himself to think of America, and the work on the farm which his aunt had promised them. He sat down on the bottom bunk next to his mother and closed his eyes and swore at himself for wanting to run away from six weeks on the ship. The ship's engines had started up and smoke swirled around the hold, making it even harder to see. He felt sick.

'It's only six weeks,' he whispered, and then stood up and picked up the blanket of food. 'We can take this up on deck with us,' he said. 'Just to be sure no one steals it.'

'I can look after your things for you.'

The small voice belonged to a very small, very old woman, lying on the bottom bunk opposite to theirs. Her white face looked like a thin wax candle in the darkness. 'I'm too weary to go up all them stairs again. There'll be time enough for that when we get there. Just put it under here.' She lifted up the blanket that hung down from her bed, covering her own few belongings. 'I'm that hungry, I'll bite anyone who goes near it.'

Julia Kelly was the old woman's name. Mammy gave her some bread from their store and they found their way up on deck again.

Four masts the great ship had, each spun with rigging like a mighty spider's web. But the *Nimrod* didn't have to wait for the wind to spring up and fill her sails. Clouds of thick, choking smoke issued from the huge chimneys at the far end of the ship, so that at first it seemed as if they had left one dark, stinking hell-hole, only to be choked by the smoke from hell-fires up on deck. But they soon discovered that when they pushed through the crowd of people to the leeward side of the

147

massive funnel, the air was so clear they could even smell the salt. Eamonn took deep breaths of fresh air.

'Where have all these people come from?' Eamonn said.

In the same instant his mother shouted above the noise of the crowd and the ship's engines, 'You wouldn't believe there were so many souls in the whole of Ireland, now would you?' She picked Shaun up and they laughed, and pushed and struggled their way through the crowds until they got to the deck railing on the side of the ship which still faced towards dry land.

'Still time to change your mind, sonny, and go back ashore,' a man joked.

Eamonn grinned, and clung tightly to the railing as a fresh surge of people crowding to get a last view of their relatives pushed him harder against it. 'Na! There's not much left for us in Ireland.'

But Kate was still in Ireland. What would happen to Kate when he had gone, if the whole of Ireland fell down with the fever? He tried to ignore the pushing and shoving behind him, searching the quay for Kate and her grandfather. They'd come all the way to Dublin to say goodbye and now they were lost in the seething masses of people waving their handkerchiefs and crying and shouting. Eamonn could have kicked himself. He had been so eager to get on board the ship that he hadn't thought to tell them where they should stand and wave.

He wished he had stayed longer ashore. It came as a surprise to him that he was so sad about leaving Ireland. 'There's nothing but ghosts back there,' he whispered, as he searched the crowds on shore for a glimpse of Kate. But he longed for the country lanes around Tullamore and the hills over Ballinglas. And then he told himself not to be stupid and forced himself to remember all the bad things that had happened. He couldn't go back. He had nowhere to go back to. The rent had run out on the room in Tullamore and there was only the workhouse and no work.

The ship was a damp, dark, stinking nightmare. Kate mustn't ever know that. Not after she had given them all her money and the chance of a new life in America.

Eamonn thought of their first sight of the ship, a graceful vessel, tracing delicate patterns on the blue sky with her wonderfully complicated masts and rigging. It was only after they had gone down into the hold in search of the prison where steerage passengers were condemned to live for the voyage, that the engines had been stoked up and the whole of the dark interior filled with choking smoke.

It was good that Kate didn't know about the ship. Eamonn looked backwards and saw the smoke from the great funnel dancing off into the sky like one more flag to give them a good send-off. Kate would see them leaving in triumph. And America would make it all worthwhile. Once they got to America everything would be all right. His mother must have guessed what he was thinking.

'Six weeks isn't so long,' she said. 'And we can always come up here, on deck, if it gets too close down there.'

Now it seemed as if everybody on the ship had had the same idea. Once again Eamonn found himself being pushed hard against the brass railing. 'Will you watch who you're pushing!' he whispered, the breath knocked out of him. But the man behind him was himself being pushed by a hundred others who had no way of stopping the stampede to the port side of the vessel.

'Move along the deck there! Move along!' boomed the voice of a giant sailor, who was lifting children up out of the crush and handing them back to the mothers who cried out when they saw them being heaved up into the air. Eamonn was moved along by the crowd until he quite lost sight of his mother and Dermot and Shaun. Panic gripped his stomach more viciously than the hunger had ever done.

The ship rolled and he watched the waves prowling

around him like a pack of wolves. They seemed to be coming closer and closer as his chest pressed harder and harder against the rail. He thought his ribs would break and he'd never breathe again. His head flopped forwards over the deck railing and the waves heaved up and down, up and down.

Eamonn tried to cry out, but he couldn't. The crowd was pressing so heavily against him that he could only look down, down the steep sides of the ship and into the hungry waves. So this was what it had all been for, all the struggling and all the hunger. He had lost his mother and Dermot and Shaun. He wouldn't find them again on a ship that was teeming with people. He'd lost Kate and her grandfather. He would never see them again.

The crowd thrust into him again like a battering ram and Eamonn was sick over the side of the ship. He would never see America. The crowd would throw him over the side and that would be the end of everything. The waves snarled up at him, worrying the side of the ship, making it heave up and down again, up and down. And it hadn't even begun to sail.

Eamonn managed to raise his head a little. He had been pushed to the far end of the ship, closest to the quay. The little, rickety houses along the lane which led down to the landing place for small boats, swayed backwards and forwards, backwards and forwards. Eamonn heard someone calling his name, but the waves growled and his head fell forward again.

He had fainted. When he opened his eyes he took a deep breath. The crowd of people had drawn right back and a sailor who looked as tall as a mast was standing over him. Eamonn closed his eyes again, eager to drift off into a sleep where he could shut out the rolling, rocking ship and the stinking hold, a sleep where he could forget that he had to search for his mother and Kate. It was easier to forget Kate than to have to stand on the deck and watch her disappear. He didn't want to leave Ireland for another nightmare. It wasn't fair. Why should he have to set out on the long journey in this coffin of a ship?

Someone said his name and he opened his eyes again and stared up at the blue summer sky. Whichever way you looked, the sky was blue, except for the few harmless, grey puffs of rain cloud steering a course from the West. Eamonn knew, as sure as night follows day, that the rain would clear and the sky would be blue again.

Then the gigantic figure of Ned Elmer, the sailor, blocked out the sky, now towering above him as high as the smoke stack in the centre of the ship, now swaying backwards and forwards with the ship. Eamonn noticed the silence. Everybody around him was so quiet that this time he distinctly heard a small voice, calling from the quay.

'Eamonn! Eamonn! Will you get up off the floor, you great lump! They'll be sailing any minute. Eamonn Kennedy! Will you get up out of that?'

'I think you're meant to be saying goodbye. There's a young lady wants you to look at her.' The sailor lifted Eamonn up on to his feet. 'No falling asleep just now. There'll be time enough for that.'

Ned helped Eamonn to the rail just as his mother and Dermot pushed their way through the crowd who had fallen right back to give him room to breathe. 'You gave me an awful fright. I thought I'd lost you for good. And then where would we be?' The only time Mammy ever scolded was when she was worried.

Eamonn steadied himself and had time to wonder at the way Shaun had fallen asleep with his head on Mammy's shoulder before he caught sight of Granddad and Kate.

'Sh! Mammy. There's Kate. And the ship's moving already.'

The ship was moving. They were going to America, after all. Eamonn had no choice any more. He would just have to see what America was like.

'You won't be sick any more now you've had your first bit of seasickness, laddy,' shouted Kate's Granddad, and laughed.

Ned Elmer waved and shouted back. 'Don't worry old man. I'll look after your grandson.'

Granddaddy laughed again and turned to smile at Kate. 'They'll always find someone. We'll have to tell your Mammy. They've got someone to look after them already. She'll feel better for that. Don't you feel better now you know they've got friends on board, my Katie?'

'No.'

Kate kept her eyes fixed on Eamonn, and he looked at her, as the ship slowly steamed out of harbour. At the mouth of the harbour the ship turned round, so that the part of the deck where Eamonn was standing with his mother and Dermot was facing directly out to sea. And Eamonn didn't look back towards Ireland again.

Kate kept her eyes fixed on the ship, and waited until it was only a grey spider's web on the horizon before she whispered, 'Don't forget to write to us.'

The ship was so far out that even if she had shouted no one on board could have heard her.

'They're daft, the lot of them. A ship of fools.'

Kate kept her eyes still fixed on the place where the ship must be, but Granddad turned round to see who had been talking. An old man, small and thin, with watery blue eyes and hair striped black and grey like a bent old badger, stood next to them, watching the ghost of a ship slide slowly out to sea.

'I mean, will you look at that lot! There's hardly a one of them on that ship can speak a word of the Queen's English and they're all dreaming as how they're going to get out there to America and everything will be as right as rain. Pah!' He spat into the harbour and started to cough. It was a long time before he finished coughing, and still Kate didn't look at him.

'To hear some of them talk, you'd think the streets was paved with gold and the President himself was going to be there to meet them in New York.' His voice was hoarse, and bitter as a bad-tasting medicine.

The old man put his hand on Kate's shoulder and whispered in her ear, 'They say they puts them all in quaramantine when they gets there. Just like animals. Puts them all in a dark room for six weeks. And if they don't go mad, it's all right. They lets them in. But then again, they're not likely to get there, if you ask me. They say there's hundreds die on the ships and gets tipped overboard.'

Kate swung round, horrified, but Granddaddy was laughing. 'Ach! Don't you believe a word of it. They'll tell you all sorts of stories.'

'It's the ones who cross the ocean as tells the stories. They're the dreamers.' The man showed a row of jagged, yellow teeth. 'They're the ones as believe in fairy stories. They're just like children, the lot of them. They think they'll be jumping off that leaking, rotten boat on the other side of the ocean and all of a sudden the world will be a better place.'

'They will too!' Kate was angry, and shook the old man's skeletal hand from her shoulder. 'They'll have a grand life out there. They'll make the world a better place.'